ONLY TO FLOAT AND LOLL ON YOUR CUSHIONS.

THE NOVELS, STORIES
AND SKETCHES OF
F. HOPKINSON SMITH

GONDOLA DAYS

CHARLES SCRIBNER'S
SONS ❧ NEW YORK ❧ 1902

CONTENTS

CHAPTER						PAGE
AN ARRIVAL	.	.	.	.	.	3
GONDOLA DAYS	.	.	.	.	.	10
ALONG THE RIVA	.	.	.	.	.	29
THE PIAZZA OF SAN MARCO	.	.	.	43
IN AN OLD GARDEN	.	.	.	.	.	59
AMONG THE FISHERMEN	.	.	.	.	86
A GONDOLA RACE	.	.	.	.	.	102
SOME VENETIAN CAFFÈS	.	.	.	.	117
ON THE HOTEL STEPS	.	.	.	.	.	127
OPEN-AIR MARKETS	.	.	.	.	137
ON RAINY DAYS	.	.	.	.	.	146
LEGACIES OF THE PAST	.	.	.	.	156
LIFE IN THE STREETS	.	.	.	.	.	177
NIGHT IN VENICE	.	.	.	.	.	197
THE GOOD GRAY NUN	.	.	.	.	206
A SUMMER'S DAY IN VENICE	.	.	.	215

v

CONTENTS

THE TOP OF A GONDOLA 223

BEHIND THE RIALTO 232

ESPERO GORGONI, GONDOLIER . . . 239

vi

ILLUSTRATIONS

ONLY TO FLOAT AND LOLL ON YOUR CUSHIONS
FROM A PHOTOGRAPH

Frontispiece

FROM DRAWINGS BY F. HOPKINSON SMITH

FACING PAGE

SOON YOU DART INTO A COOL CANAL . . .
AND REST AT A LOW STEP . . . 22

ONE UP A NARROW CANAL . . . 40

GONDOLA DAYS

AN ARRIVAL

YOU really begin to arrive in Venice when you leave Milan. Your train is hardly out of the station before you have conjured up all the visions and traditions of your childhood: great rows of white palaces running sheer into the water; picture-book galleys reflected upside down in red lagoons; domes and minarets, kiosks, towers, and steeples, queer-arched temples, and the like.

As you speed on in the dusty train, your memory - fed imagination takes new flights. You expect gold-incrusted barges, hung with Persian carpets, rowed by slaves double-banked, and trailing rare brocades in a sea of China-blue, to meet you at the water-landing.

By the time you reach Verona your mental panorama makes another turn. The very name suggests the gay lover of the *bal masqué*, the poisoned vial, and the calcium moonlight illuminating the wooden tomb of the stage-set graveyard. You instinctively look around for the fair Juliet and her nurse. There are half a

3

dozen as pretty Veronese, attended by their watchful duennas, going down by train to the City by the Sea ; but they do not satisfy you. You want one in a tight-fitting white satin gown with flowing train, a diamond-studded girdle, and an ostrich-plume fan. The nurse, too, must be stouter, and have a high-keyed voice ; be bent a little in the back, and shake her finger in a threatening way, as in the old mezzotints you have seen of Mrs. Siddons or Peg Woffington. This pair of Dulcineas on the seat in front, in silk dusters, with a lunch-basket and a box of sweets, are too modern and commonplace for you, and will not do.

When you roll into Padua, and neither doge nor inquisitor in ermine or black gown boards the train, you grow restless. A deadening suspicion enters your mind. What if, after all, there should be no Venice ? Just as there is no Robinson Crusoe nor man Friday ; no stockade, nor little garden : no Shahrazad telling her stories far into the Arabian night; no Santa Claus with reindeer ; no Rip Van Winkle haunted by queer little gnomes in fur caps. As this suspicion deepens, the blood clogs in your veins, and a thousand shivers go down your spine. You begin to fear that all these traditions of your childhood, all these dreams and fancies, are like

4

the thousand and one other lies that have been told to and believed by you since the days when you spelled out words in two syllables.

Upon leaving Mestre — the last station — you smell the salt air of the Adriatic through the open car window. Instantly your hopes revive. Craning your head far out, you catch a glimpse of a long, low, monotonous bridge, and away off in the purple haze, the dreary outline of a distant city. You sink back into your seat exhausted. Yes, you knew it all the time. The whole thing is a swindle and a sham !

" All out for Venice," says the guard, in French.

Half a dozen porters — well dressed, civil-spoken porters, flat-capped and numbered — seize your traps and help you from the train. You look up. It is like all the rest of the depots since you left Paris, — high, dingy, besmoked, beraftered, beglazed, and be ——— ! No, you are past all that. You are not angry. You are merely broken-hearted. Another idol of your childhood shattered ; another coin that your soul coveted, nailed to the wall of your experience — a counterfeit !

" This door to the gondolas," says the porter. He is very polite. If he were less so, you might make excuse to brain him on the way out.

The depot ends in a narrow passageway. It is the same old fraud, — custom-house officers on each side ; man with a punch mutilating tickets ; rows of other men with brass medals on their arms the size of apothecaries' scales — hackmen, you think, with their whips outside — licensed runners for the gondoliers, you learn afterward. They are all shouting — all intent on carrying you off bodily. The vulgar modern horde !

Soon you begin to breathe more easily. There is another door ahead, framing a bit of blue sky. "At least, the sun shines here," you say to yourself. "Thank God for that !"

"This way, signore."

One step, and you stand in the light. Now look ! Below, at your very feet, a great flight of marble steps drops down to the water's edge. Crowding these steps is a throng of gondoliers, porters, women with fans and gay - colored gowns, priests, fruit-sellers, water-carriers, and pedlers. At the edge, and away over as far as the beautiful marble church, a flock of gondolas like black swans curve in and out. Beyond stretches the double line of church and palace, bordering the glistening highway. Over all is the soft golden haze, the shimmer, the translucence of the Venetian summer sunset.

AN ARRIVAL

With your head in a whirl, — so intense is the surprise, so foreign to your traditions and dreams the actuality, — you throw yourself on the yielding cushions of a waiting gondola. A turn of the gondolier's wrist, and you dart into a narrow canal. Now the smells greet you, — damp, cool, low-tide smells. The palaces and warehouses shut out the sky. On you go — under low bridges of marble, fringed with people leaning listlessly over; around sharp corners, their red and yellow bricks worn into ridges by thousands of rounding boats; past open plazas crowded with the teeming life of the city. The shadows deepen; the waters glint like flakes of broken gold leaf. High up in an opening you catch a glimpse of a tower, rose-pink in the fading light; it is the Campanile. Farther on, you slip beneath an arch caught between two palaces and held in mid air. You look up, shuddering as you trace the outlines of the fatal Bridge of Sighs. For a moment all is dark. Then you glide into a sea of opal, of amethyst and sapphire.

The gondola stops near a small flight of stone steps protected by huge poles striped with blue and red. Other gondolas are debarking. A stout porter in gold lace steadies yours as you alight.

7

"Monsieur's rooms are quite ready. They are over the garden ; the one with the balcony overhanging the water.''

The hall is full of people (it is the Britannia, the best hotel in Venice), grouped about the tables, chatting or reading, sipping coffee or eating ices. Beyond, from an open door, comes the perfume of flowers. You pass out, cross a garden, cool and fresh in the darkening shadows, and enter a small room opening on a staircase. You walk up and through the cosey apartments, push back a folding glass door, and step out upon a balcony of marble.

How still it all is ! Only the plash of the water about the bows of the gondolas, and the little waves snapping at the water-steps. Even the groups of people around the small iron tables below, partly hidden by the bloom of oleanders, talk in half-heard whispers.

You look about you, — the stillness filling your soul, the soft air embracing you, — out over the blossoms of the oleanders, across the shimmering water, beyond the beautiful dome of the Salute, glowing like a huge pearl in the clear evening light. No, it is not the Venice of your childhood ; not the dream of your youth. It is softer, more mellow, more restful, more exquisite in its harmonies.

8

AN ARRIVAL

Suddenly a strain of music breaks upon your ear — a soft, low strain. Nearer it comes, nearer. You lean forward over the marble rail to catch its meaning. Far away across the surface of the beautiful sea floats a tiny boat. Every swing of the oar leaves in its wake a quivering thread of gold. Now it rounds the great red buoy, and is lost behind the sails of a lazy lugger drifting with the tide. Then the whole broad water rings with the melody. In another instant it is beneath you — the singer standing, holding his hat for your pennies; the chorus seated, with upturned, expectant faces.

Into the empty hat you pour all your store of small coins, your eyes full of tears.

GONDOLA DAYS

THAT first morning in Venice! It is the summer, of course — never the winter. This beautiful bride of the sea is loveliest when bright skies bend tenderly over her, when white mists fall softly around her, and the lagoons about her feet are sheets of burnished silver; when the red oleanders thrust their blossoms exultingly above the low, crumbling walls; when the black hoods of winter *félzi* are laid by at the *traghetti*, and gondolas flaunt their white awnings; when the melon-boats, with lifeless sails, drift lazily by, and the shrill cry of the fruit-vender floats over the water; when the air is steeped, permeated, soaked through and through with floods of sunlight — quivering, brilliant, radiant; sunlight that blazes from out a sky of pearl and opal and sapphire; sunlight that drenches every old palace with liquid amber, kissing every moulding awake, and soothing every shadow to sleep; sunlight that caresses and does not scorch, that dazzles and does not blind, that illumines, irradiates, makes glorious, every sail and tower and dome, from the instant the great god of the east shakes the dripping waters of the Adriatic from his face until he sinks behind the purple hills of Padua.

These mornings, then! How your heart warms and your blood tingles when you remember that first one in Venice — your first day in a gondola!

You recall that you were leaning upon your balcony overlooking the garden when you caught sight of your gondolier; the gondolier whom Joseph, prince among porters, had engaged for you the night of your arrival.

On that first morning you were just out of your bed. In fact, you had hardly been in it all night. You had fallen asleep in a whirl of contending emotions. Half a dozen times you had been up and out on this balcony, suddenly aroused by the passing of some music-boat filling the night with a melody that seemed a thousandfold more enchanting because of your sudden awakening, — the radiant moon, and the glistening water beneath. I say you were out again upon this same balcony overlooking the oleanders, the magnolias, and the palms. You heard the tinkling of spoons in the cups below, and knew that some earlier riser was taking his coffee in the dense shrubbery; but it made no impression upon you. Your eye was fixed on the beautiful dome of the Salute opposite; on the bronze goddess of the Dogana waving her veil in the soft air; on the group of lighters moored to the quay, their red and yellow sails aglow; on the noble tower of San Giorgio, sharp cut against the glory of the east.

Now you catch a waving hand and the lifting of a cap on the gravel walk below. " At what hour will the signore want the gondola ?"

You remember the face, brown and sunny, the eyes laughing, the curve of the black mustache, and how the wavy short hair curled about his neck and struggled out from under his cap. He has on another suit, newly starched and snow white; a loose shirt, a wide collar trimmed with blue, and duck trousers. Around his waist is a wide blue sash, the ends hanging to his knees. About his throat is a loose silk scarf, — so loose that you note the broad, manly chest, the muscles of the neck half concealed by the cross-barred boating-shirt covering the brown skin.

There is a cheeriness, a breeziness, a spring about this young fellow that inspires you. As you look down into his face you feel that he is part of the air, of the sunshine, of the perfume of the oleanders. He belongs to everything about him, and everything belongs to him. His costume, his manner, the very way he holds his hat, show you at a glance that while for the time being he is your servant, he is, in many things deeply coveted by you, greatly your master. If you had his chest and his forearm, his sunny temper, his perfect digestion and contentment, you could easily spare one half of your world's belongings in payment. When you have lived a month with him and have caught the spirit of the man, you will forget all about these several relations of servant and master. The six francs a day that you pay him will seem only your own contribution to the support of the gondola ; his share being his services. When you have spent half the night at the Lido, he swimming at your side, or have rowed all the way to Torcello, or have heard early mass at San Rosario, away up the Giudecca, he kneeling before you, his hat on the cool pavement next your own, you will begin to lose sight even of the francs, and want to own gondola and all yourself, that you may make *him* guest and thus discharge somewhat the ever-increasing obligation of hospitality under which he places you. Soon you will begin to realize that despite your belongings — wealth to this gondolier beyond his wildest dreams — he

13

in reality is the richer of the two. He has in-
herited all this glory of palace, sea, and sky,
from the day of his birth, and can live in it
every hour in the year, with no fast-ebbing letter of credit nor near-approaching sailing day to
sadden his soul or poison the cup of his pleasure. When your fatal day comes and your
trunk is packed, he will stand at the water-stairs
of the station, hat in hand, the tears in his eyes;
and when one of the demons of the master
spirit of the age — Hurry — has tightened its
grip upon you and you are whirled out and
across the great iron bridge, and you begin once
more the life that now you loathe, even before
you have reached Mestre — if your gondolier
is like my own gondolier, Espero, my Espero
Gorgoni, whom I love — you would find him
on his knees in the church next the station,
whispering a prayer for your safe journey across
the sea, and spending one of your miserable
francs for some blessed candles to burn until you
reached home.

But you have not answered your gondolier,
who stands with upturned eyes on the gravelled
walk below.

" At what hour will the signore want the
gondola ? "

You awake from your reverie. Now ! as soon

as you swallow your coffee. Ten minutes later you bear your weight on Giorgio's bent elbow and step into his boat.

It is like nothing else of its kind your feet have ever touched — so yielding and yet so firm; so shallow and yet so stanch; so light, so buoyant, and so welcoming to peace and rest and comfort!

How daintily it sits the water! How like a knowing swan it bends its head, the iron blade of the bow, and glides out upon the bosom of the Grand Canal! You stop for a moment, noting the long, narrow body, blue-black and silver in the morning light, as graceful in its curves as a bird; the white awning amidships draped at sides and back, the softly yielding, morocco-covered seat, all cushions and silk fringes, and the silken cords curbing quaint lions of polished brass. Beyond and aft stands your gondolier, with easy, graceful swing bending to his oar. You stoop down, part the curtains, and sink into the cushions. Suddenly an air of dignified importance steals over you. Never in your whole life have you been so magnificently carried about. Four-in-hands, commodores' gigs, landaus in triumphant processions with white horses and plumes, seem tame and commonplace. Here is a whole barge, galleon,

Bucentaur, all to yourself, — noiseless, alert, subservient to your airiest whim, obedient to the lightest touch. You float between earth and sky. You feel like a potentate out for an airing, housed like a Rajah, served like Cleopatra, and rowed like a Doge. You command space and dominate the elements.

But Giorgio is leaning on his oar, millions of diamonds dripping from its blade.

"Where now, signore ?"

Anywhere, so he keeps in the sunlight. To the Piazza, perhaps, and then around San Giorgio with its red tower and noble façade, and later, when the shadows lengthen, away down to the Public Garden, and home again in the twilight by way of the Giudecca.

This gondola landing of the Piazza, the most important of the cab-stands in Venice, is the stepping-stone — a wet and ooze-covered stone — to the heart of the city. Really the heart, for the very life of every canal, *campo*, and street courses through it in unending flow all the livelong day and night, from the earliest blush of dawn to the earliest blush of dawn again ; no one ever seems to go to bed in Venice. Along and near the edge of this landing stand the richest examples of Venetian architecture. First, the Royal Gardens of the king's palace, with its

16

balustrade of marble and broad flight of water-steps ; then the Library, with its cresting of statues, white against the sky ; then the two noble columns, the gateless posts of the Piazzetta, bearing Saint Theodore and the Lion of Venice ; and beyond, past the edge of San Marco, the clock tower and the three great flag-staffs; then the Palace of the Doges, that master work of the fifteenth century ; then the prison, with a glimpse of the Bridge of Sighs caught in mid air; then the great scimitar-sweep of the Riva, its point lost in the fringe of trees shading the Public Garden ; and then, over all, as you look up, the noble Campanile, the wonderful bell tower of San Marco, unadorned, simple, majestic — up, up, into the still air, its gilded angel, life-size, with outstretched wings flashing in the morning sun, a mere dot of gold against the blue.

Before you touch the lower steps of the water-stairs, your eye falls upon an old man with bared head. He holds a long staff studded with bad coins, having a hook at one end. With this in one hand he steadies your gondola, with the other he holds out his hat. He is an aged gondolier, too old now to row. He knows you, the poor fellow, and he knows your kind. How many such enthusiasts has he helped to alight !

17

And he knows Giorgio too, and remembers when, like him, he bent his oar with the best. You drop a penny into his wrinkled hand, catch his grateful thanks, and join the throng. The arcades under the Library are full of people smoking and sipping coffee. How delicious the aroma and the pungent smell of tobacco! In the shadow of the Doges' Palace groups idle and talk, —a little denser in spots where some artist has his easel up, or some pretty, dainty child is feeding the pigeons.

A moment more and you are in the Piazza of San Marco ; the grand piazza of the doges, with its thousands of square feet of white pavement blazing in the sun, framed on three sides by marble palaces, dominated by the noblest campanile on the globe, and enriched, glorified, made inexpressibly precious and unique by that jewel in marble, in porphyry, in verd antique and bronze, that despair of architects of to-day, that delight of the artists of all time — the most sacred, the church of San Marco.

In and out this great quadrangle whirl the pigeons, the pigeons of Dandolo, up into the soft clouds, the light flashing from their throats ; sifting down in showers on gilded cross and rounded dome ; clinging to intricate carvings, over and under the gold-crowned heads of saints in stone and bronze ; across the baking plaza in flurries of gray and black ; resting like a swarm of flies, only to startle, mass, and swirl again. Pets of the state, these birds, since the siege of Candia, when the great Admiral Dandolo's chief bearer of dispatches, the ancestor of one of these same white-throated doves, brought the good news to Venice the day the admiral's victorious banner was thrown to the breeze, and the Grand Council, sitting in state, first learned the tidings from the soft plumage of its wings.

At one end, fronting the church, stand the three great flagpoles, the same you saw at the landing, socketed in bronze, exquisitely modelled and chased, bearing the banners of Candia, Cyprus, and the Morea — kingdoms conquered by the state — all three in a row, presenting arms to the power that overthrew them, and forever dipping their colors to the glory of its past.

Here, too, in this noble square, under your very feet, what solemnities, what historic fêtes, what conspiracies ! Here for centuries has been held the priestly pageant of Corpus Christi, aflame with lanterns and flambeaux. Here eleven centuries ago blind old Dandolo received the Crusader chiefs of France. Here the splendid nuptials of Francesco Foscari were celebrated by a tournament witnessed by thirty thousand people, and lasting ten days. Here the conspiracies of Tiepolo and Faliero were crushed — Venetian against Venetian the only time in a thousand years. And here Italy suffered her crowning indignity, the occupation by the French under the newly fledged warrior who unlimbered his cannon at the door of the holy church, pushed the four bronze horses from their pedestals over the sacred entrance, — the horses of Constantine, wrought by Lysippus the Greek, — despoiled the noble church of its silver lamps, robbed the ancient column of its winged lion, and then, after a campaign unprecedented in its brilliancy, unexampled in the humiliation and degradation it entailed upon a people who for ten centuries had known no power outside of Venice, planted in the centre of this same noble square, with an irony as bitter as it was cruel, the "Tree of Liberty," at which was burned, on the 4th of June, 1797, the insignia of the ancient republic.

And yet, notwithstanding all her vicissitudes, the Venice of to-day is still the Venice of her glorious past, the Venice of Dandolo, Foscari, and Faliero. The actors are long since dead, but the stage setting is the same, — the same sun, the same air, the same sky over all. The beautiful dome of the Salute still dominates the Grand Canal. The great plaza is still perfect in all its proportions and in all that made up its beauty and splendor. The Campanile still raises its head, glistening in the morning light. High over all still flash and swoop the pigeons of Venice — the pigeons of Dandolo — now black as cinders, now flakes of gold in the yellow light. The doors of the sacred church are still open ; the people pass in and out. Under the marble arcades, where the soldiers of the army of France stacked their arms, to-day sit hundreds of free Venetians, with their wives and sweethearts, sipping their ices and coffee ; the great orchestra, the king's band, filling the air with its music.

When you ask what magician has wrought this change, let the old guide answer as once he answered me when, crossing the Piazza and uncovering his head, he pointed to a stone and said, in his soft Italian, —

"Here, signore, — just here, where the great Napoleon burnt our flag, — the noble republic of our fathers, under our good king and his royal spouse, was born anew."

But you cannot stay. You will return and study the Piazza to-morrow ; not now. The air intoxicates you. The sunlight is in your blood ; your cheeks burn ; you look out and over the Grand Canal — molten silver in the shimmer of the morning. Below, near the Public Garden, beyond San Giorgio, like a cluster of butterflies, hovers a fleet of Chioggia fishing-boats, becalmed in the channel. Off the Riva, near Danieli's, lies the Trieste steamer, just arrived, a swarm of gondolas and *barche* about her landing-ladders ; the yellow smoke of her funnel drifting lazily. Farther away, on the golden ball of the Dogana, the bronze Goddess of the Wind poises light as air, her face aflame, her whirling sail bent with the passing breeze.

You resolve to stop no more ; only to float, loll on your cushions, watch the gulls circle, and the slow sweep of the oars of the luggers. You would throw open — wide open — the great swinging gates of your soul. You not only would enjoy, you would absorb, drink in, fill yourself to the brim.

For hours you drift about. There is plenty of time to-morrow for the churches and palaces and caffès. To-day you want only the salt air in your face, the splash and gurgle of the water at the bow, and the low song that Giorgio sings to himself as he bends to his blade.

Soon you dart into a cool canal, skirt along an old wall, water-stained and worn, and rest at

22

SOON YOU DART INTO A COOL CANAL . . . AND REST AT A LOW STEP

a low step. Giorgio springs out, twists a cord around an iron ring, and disappears through an archway framing a garden abloom with flowering vines.

It is high noon. Now for your midday luncheon!

You have had all sorts of breakfasts offered you in your wanderings: On white-winged yachts, with the decks scoured clean, the brass glistening, the awning overhead. In the wilderness, lying on balsam boughs, the smell of the bacon and crisping trout filling the bark slant, the blue smoke wreathing the tall pines. In the gardens of Sunny Spain — one you remember at Granada, hugging the great wall of the Alhambra — you see the table now with its heap of fruit and flowers, and can hear the guitar of the gypsy behind the pomegranate. Along the shore of the beautiful bay of Matanzas, where the hidalgo who had watched you paint swept down in his *volante* and carried you off to his oranges and omelette. At St. Cloud, along the Seine, with the noiseless waiter in the seedy dress suit and necktie of the night before. But the *filet* and melon! Yes, you would go again. I say you have had all sorts of breakfasts out of doors in your time, but never yet in a gondola.

A few minutes later Giorgio pushes aside the vines. He carries a basket covered with a white cloth. This he lays at your feet on the floor of the boat. You catch sight of the top of a siphon and a flagon of wine ; do not hurry, wait till he serves it. But not here, where anybody might come ; farther down, where the oleanders hang over the wall, their blossoms in the water, and where the air blows cool between the overhanging palaces.

Later Giorgio draws all the curtains except at the side next the oleanders, steps aft and fetches a board, which he rests on the little side seats in front of your lounging - cushions. On this board he spreads the cloth, and then the seltzer and Chianti, the big glass of powdered ice and the little hard Venetian rolls. (By the bye, do you know that there is only one form of primitive roll, the world over ?) Then come the cheese, the Gorgonzola — active, alert Gorgonzola, all green spots — wrapped in a leaf ; a rough - jacketed melon, with some figs and peaches. Last of all, away down in the bottom of the basket, there is a dish of macaroni garnished with peppers. You do not want any meat. If you did you would not get it. Some time when you are out on the canal, or up the Giudecca, you might get a fish freshly broiled

24

from a passing cook-boat serving the watermen —a sort of floating kitchen for those who are too poor for a fire of their own — but never meat.

Giorgio serves you as daintily as would a woman, — unfolding the cheese, splitting the rolls, parting the melon into crescents, flecking off each seed with his knife ; and last, the coffee from the little copper coffee-pot, and the thin cakes of sugar, in the thick, unbreakable, dumpy little cups.

There are no courses in this repast. You light a cigarette with your first mouthful and smoke straight through : it is that kind of breakfast.

Then you spread yourself over space, flat on your back, the smoke curling out through the half-drawn curtains. Soon your gondolier gathers up the fragments, half a melon and the rest, — there is always enough for two, — moves aft, and you hear the clink of the glass and the swish of the siphon. Later you note the closely eaten crescents floating by, and the empty leaf. Giorgio was hungry too.

But the garden ! there is time for that. You soon discover that it is unlike any other you know. There are no flower-beds and gravel walks, and no brick fountains with the scantily dressed cast-iron boy struggling with the green painted dolphin, the water spurting from its open mouth. There is water, of course, but it is down a deep well with a great coping of marble, encircled by exquisite carvings and mellow with mould; and there are low trellises of grapes, and a tangle of climbing roses half concealing a weather-stained Cupid with a broken arm. And there is an old-fashioned sun-dial, and sweet-smelling box cut into fantastic shapes, and a nest of an arbor so thickly matted with leaves and interlaced branches that you think of your Dulcinea at once. And there are marble benches and stone steps, and at the farther end an old rusty gate through which Giorgio brought the luncheon.

It is all so new to you, and so cool and rest-ful! For the first time you begin to realize that you are breathing the air of a City of Silence. No hum of busy loom, no tramp of horse or rumble of wheel, no jar or shock; only the voices that come over the water, and the plash of the ripples as you pass. But the day is wan-ing; into the sunlight once more!

Giorgio is fast asleep; his arm across his face, his great broad chest bared to the sky.

" Si, signore ! "

He is up in an instant, rubbing the sleep from his eyes, catching his oar as he springs.

You glide in and out again, under marble bridges thronged with people ; along quays lined with boats ; by caffè, church, and palace, and so on to the broad water of the Public Garden.

But you do not land ; some other day for that. You want the row back up the canal, with the glory of the setting sun in your face. Suddenly, as you turn, the sun is shut out : it is the great warship Stromboli, lying at anchor off the garden wall ; huge, solid as a fort, fine-lined as a yacht, with exquisite detail of rail, mast, yardarms, and gun mountings, the light flashing from her polished brasses.

In a moment you are under her stern, and beyond, skirting the old shipyard with the cu-rious arch, — the one Whistler etched, — sheer-ing to avoid the little steamers puffing with modern pride, their noses high in air at the gondolas ; past the long quay of the Riva, where the torpedo-boats lie tethered in a row, like swift horses eager for a dash ; past the fruit-boats dropping their sails for a short cut to the market next the Rialto ; past the long, low, ugly bath-house anchored off the Dogana ; past the wonderful, the matchless, the never to be unloved or forgotten, the most blessed, the Santa Maria della Salute.

Oh ! this drift back, square in the face of the

royal sun, attended by all the pomp and glory of a departing day! What shall be said of this revelling, rioting, dominant god of the west, clothed in purple and fine gold; strewing his path with rose leaves thrown broadcast on azure fields; rolling on beds of violet; saturated, steeped, drunken with color; every steeple, tower, and dome ablaze; the whole world on tiptoe, kissing its hands good-night!

Giorgio loves it too. His cap is off, lying on the narrow deck; his cravat loosened, his white shirt, as he turns up the Giudecca, flashing like burning gold.

Somehow you cannot sit and take your ease in the fulness of all this beauty and grandeur. You spring to your feet. You must see behind and on both sides, your eye roving eagerly away out to the lagoon beyond the great flour-mill and the gardens.

Suddenly a delicate violet light falls about you; the lines of palaces grow purple; the water is dulled to a soft gray, broken by long, undulating waves of blue; the hulls of the fishing-boats become inky black, their listless sails deepening in the falling shadows. Only the little cupola high up on the dome of the Redentore still burns pink and gold. Then it fades and is gone. The day is done!

ALONG THE RIVA

THE afternoon hours are always the best. In the morning the great sweep of dazzling pavement is a blaze of white light, spotted with moving dots of color. These dots carry gay-colored parasols and fans, or shield their eyes with aprons, hugging, as they scurry along, the half shadows of a bridge-rail or caffè awning. Here and there, farther down along the Riva, are larger dots — fruit-sellers crouching under huge umbrellas, or groups of gondoliers under improvised awnings of sailcloth and boat oars. Once in a while one of these water cabmen darts out from his shelter like an old spider, waylays a bright fly as she hurries past, and carries her off bodily to his gondola. Should she escape he crawls back again lazily and is merged once more in the larger dot. In the noonday glare even these disappear; the fruit-sellers seeking some shaded *calle*, the gondoliers the cool coverings of their boats.

Now that the Sun God has chosen to hide his face behind the trees of the King's Garden, this blaze of white is toned to a cool gray. Only San Giorgio's tower across the Grand Canal is aflame, and that but halfway down its bright red length. The people, too, who have been all day behind closed blinds and doors, are astir. The awnings of the caffès are thrown back and the windows of the balconies opened. The waiters bring out little tables, arranging the chairs in rows like those in a concert hall. The boatmen who have been asleep under cool bridges, curled up on the decks of their boats, stretch themselves awake, rubbing their eyes. The churches swing back their huge doors, — even the red curtains of the Chiesa della Pietá are caught to one side, so that you can see the sickly yellow glow of the candles far back on the altars and smell the incense as you pass.

Soon the current from away up near the Piazza begins to flow down towards the Public Garden, which lies at the end of this Grand Promenade of Venice. Priests come, and students ; sailors on a half day's leave ; stevedores from the salt warehouses ; fishermen ; pedlers, with knickknacks and sweetmeats ; throngs from the hotels ; and slender, graceful Venetians, out for their afternoon stroll in twos and threes, with high combs and gay shawls, worn as a Spanish donna would her mantilla — bewitching creatures in cool muslin dresses and wide sashes of silk, with restless butterfly fans, and restless, wicked eyes too, that flash and coax as they saunter along.

Watch those officers wheel and turn. See how they laugh when they meet. What confidences under mustachios and fans! Half an hour from now you will find the four at Florian's, as happy over a little cherry juice and water as if it were the dryest of all the Extras. Later on, away out beyond San Giorgio, four cigarettes could light for you their happy faces, the low plash of their gondolier's oar keeping time to the soft notes of a guitar.

Yes, one must know the Riva in the afternoon. I know it every hour in the day, though I love it most in the cool of its shadows. And I know every caffè, church, and palace along its whole length, from the Molo to the garden. And I know the bridges, too; best of all the one below the Arsenal, the Veneta Marina, and the one you cross before reaching the little church that stands aside as if to let you pass, and the queer-shaped Piazzetta beyond, with the flagpole and marble balustrade. And I know that old wine shop where the chairs and tables are drawn close up to the very bridge itself, its awnings half over the last step.

My own gondolier, Espero — bless his sunny face! — knows the owner of this shop and has known her for years; a great, superb creature, with eyes that flash and smoulder under heaps of tangled black hair. He first presented me to this grand duchess of the Riva years ago, when I wanted a dish of macaroni browned on a shallow plate. Whenever I turn in now out of the heat for a glass of crushed ice and orange juice, she mentions the fact and points with pride to the old earthen platter. It is nearly burnt through with my many toastings.

But the bridge is my delight; the arch underneath is so cool, and I have darted under it so often for luncheon and half an hour's siesta! On these occasions the old burnt-bottomed dish is brought to my gondola sizzling hot, with coffee and rolls, and sometimes a bit of broiled fish as an extra touch.

This bridge has always been the open-air clubroom of the entire neighborhood, — everybody who has any lounging to do is a life member. All day long its *habitués* hang over it, gazing listlessly out upon the lagoon; singly, in bunches, in swarms when the fish-boats round in from Chioggia, or a new P. and O. steamer arrives. Its hand-rail of broad marble is polished smooth by the arms and legs and blue overalls of two centuries.

There is also a very dear friend of mine living near this bridge, whom you might as well know before I take another step along the Riva. He is attached to my suite. I have a large following quite of his kind, scattered all over Venice. As I am on my way, in this chapter, to the Public Garden, and can never get past this his favorite haunt without his cheer and laugh to greet me, so I cannot, if I would, avoid bringing him in now, knowing full well that he would bring himself in — and unannounced — whenever it should please his excellency so to do. He is a happy-hearted, devil-may-care young fellow, who haunts this particular vicinity, and who has his bed and board wherever, at the moment, he may happen to be. The bed problem never troubles him ; a bit of sailcloth under the shadow of the hand-rail will do, or a straw mat behind the angle of a wall, or even what shade I can spare from my own white umbrella, with the hard marble flags for feathers. The item of board is a trifle, yet only a trifle, more serious. It may be a fragment of polenta, or a couple of figs, or only a drink from the copper bucket of some passing girl. Quantity, quality, and time of serving are immaterial to him.

33

There will be something to eat before night, and it always comes. One of the pleasures of the neighborhood is to share with him a bite.

This beggar, tramp, *lasagnone*, ragged, barefooted, and sunbrowned, would send a flutter through the hearts of a matinée full of pretty girls, could he step to the footlights just as he is, and with his superb baritone voice ring out one of his own native songs. Lying as he does now under my umbrella, his broad chest burnt almost black, the curls glistening about his forehead, his well-trimmed mustache curving around a mouth half open, shading a row of teeth white as milk, his Leporello hat thrown aside, a broad red sash girding his waist, the fine muscles of his thighs filling his overalls, these same pretty girls might perhaps only draw their skirts aside as they passed : environment plays such curious tricks.

This friend of mine, this royal pauper, Luigi, never in the recollection of any mortal man or woman was known to do a stroke of work. He lives somewhere up a crooked canal, with an old mother who adores him — as, in fact, does every other woman he knows, young or old — and whose needle keeps together the rags that only accentuate more clearly the superb lines of his figure. And yet one cannot call him

34

a burden on society. On the contrary, Luigi has especial duties which he never neglects. Every morning at sunrise he is out on the bridge watching the Chioggia boats as they beat up past the Garden trying to make the red buoy in the channel behind San Giorgio, and enlarging on their seagoing qualities to an admiring group of bystanders. At noon he is plumped down in the midst of a bevy of wives and girls, flat on the pavement, his back against a doorway in some courtyard. The wives mend and patch, the girls string beads, and the children play around on the marble flagging, Luigi monopolizing all the talk and conducting all the gayety, the whole coterie listening. He makes love, and chaffs, and sings, and weaves romances, until the inquisitive sun peeps into the *patio;* then he is up and out on the bridge again, and so down the Riva, with the grace of an Apollo and the air of a thoroughbred.

When I think of all the sour tempers in the world, all the people with weak backs and chests and limbs, all the dyspeptics, all the bad livers and worse hearts, all the mean people and the sordid, all those who pose as philanthropists, professing to ooze sunshine and happiness from their very pores; all the downtrodden and the economical ones; all those on

35

half pay and no work, and those on full pay and no work, and those on full pay and too little — and then look at this magnificent condensation of bone, muscle, and sinew ; this Greek god of a tramp, unselfish, good-tempered, sunny-hearted, wanting nothing, having everything, envying nobody, happy as a lark, one continuous song all the day long; ready to catch a line, to mind a child, to carry a pail of water for any old woman, from the fountain in the Campo near by to the top of any house, no matter how high, — when, I say, I think of this prince of good fellows leading his Adam-before-the-fall sort of existence, I seriously consider the advisability of my pensioning him for the remainder of his life on one *lira* a day, a fabulous sum to him, merely to be sure that nothing in the future will ever spoil his temper and so rob me of the ecstasy of knowing and of being always able to find one supremely happy human creature on this earth.

But as I have said, I am on my way to the Public Garden. Everybody else is going too. Step to the marble balustrade of this three-cornered Piazzeta and see if the prows of the gondolas are not all pointed that way. I am afoot, have left the Riva and am strolling down the Via Garibaldi, the widest street in Venice.

There are no palaces here, only a double row of shops, their upper windows and balconies festooned with drying clothes, their doors choked with piles of fruit and merchandise. A little farther down is a marble bridge, and then the arching trees of the biggest and breeziest sweep of green in all Venice, — the Giardini Pubblici, — many acres in extent, bounded by a great wall surmounted by a marble balustrade more than a mile in length, and thickly planted with sycamores and flowering shrubs. Its water front commands the best view of the glory of a Venetian sunset.

This garden, for Venice, is really a very modern kind of public garden, after all. It was built in the beginning of the present century, about 1810, when the young Corsican directed one Giovanni Antonio Selva to demolish a group of monasteries encumbering the ground and from their débris to construct the foundations of this noble park, with its sea wall, landings, and triumphal gate.

Whenever I stretch myself out under the grateful shade of these splendid trees, I always forgive the Corsican for robbing San Marco of its bronze horses and for riding his own up the incline of the Campanile, and even for levelling the monasteries.

And the Venetians of to-day are grateful too, however much their ancestors may have reviled the conqueror for his vandalism. All over its gravelled walks you will find them lolling on the benches, grouped about the pretty caffès, taking their coffee or eating ices ; leaning by the hour over the balustrade and watching the boats and little steamers. The children romp and play, the candy man and the sellers of sweet cakes ply their trade, and the vender with cool drinks stands over his curious four-legged tray, studded with bits of brass and old coins, and calls out his several mixtures. The officers are here, too, twisting their mustachios and fingering their cigarettes ; fine ladies saunter along, preceded by their babies, half smothered in lace and borne on pillows in the arms of Italian peasants with red cap-ribbons touching the ground ; and barefooted, frowzy-headed girls from the rookeries behind the Arsenal idle about, four or five abreast, their arms locked, mocking the sailors and filling the air with laughter.

Then there are a menagerie, or rather some wire-fenced paddocks filled with kangaroos and rabbits, and an aviary of birds, and a big casino where the band plays, and where for half a *lira*, some ten cents, you can see a variety performance without the variety, and hear these light-hearted people laugh to their hearts' content.

And last of all, away down at one end, near the wall fronting the church of San Giuseppe, there lives in miserable solitude the horse— the only horse in Venice. He is not always the same horse. A few years ago, when I first knew him, he was a forlorn, unkempt, lonely looking quadruped of a dark brown color, and with a threadbare tail. When I saw him last, within the year, he was a hand higher, white, and wore a caudal appendage with a pronounced bang. Still he is the same horse — Venice never affords but one. When not at work (he gathered leaves in the old days ; now I am ashamed to say he operates a lawn mower as well), he leans his poor old tired head listlessly over the rail, refusing the cakes the children offer him. At these times he will ruminate by the hour over his unhappy lot. When the winter comes, and there are no more leaves to rake, no gravel to haul, nor grass to mow, they lead him down to the gate opening on the little side canal and push him aboard a flat scow, and so on up the Grand Canal and across the lagoon to Mestre. As he passes along, looking helplessly from side to side, the gondoliers revile him and the children jeer at him, and those on the little steamboats pelt him with peach pits, cigar ends, and bits of broken coal. Poor old Rosinante, there is no page in the history of Venice which your ancestors helped glorify !

There are two landings along the front of the garden, — one below the west corner, up a narrow canal, and the other midway of the long sea wall, where all the gondolas load and unload. You know this last landing at once. Ziem has painted it over and over again for a score of years or more, and this master of color is still at it. With him it is a strip of brilliant red, a background of autumn foliage, and a creamy flight of steps running down to a sea of deepest ultramarine. There is generally a mass of fishing-boats, too, in brilliant colorings, moored to the wall, and a black gondola for a centre-dark.

When you row up to this landing to-day, you are surprised to find it all sunshine and glitter. The trees are fresh and crisp, the marble is dazzling white, and the water sparkling and limpid with gray-green tints. But please do not criticise Ziem. You do not see it his way, but that is not his fault. Venice is a hundred different Venices to as many different painters. If it were not so, you would not be here to-day, nor love it as you do. Besides, when you think it all over, you will admit that Ziem, of all living

ONE . . . UP A NARROW CANAL.

painters, has best rendered its sensuous, color-soaked side. And yet, when you land, you wonder why the colorist did not bring his easel closer and give you a nearer view of this superb water-landing, with the crowds of gayly dressed people, swarms of gondolas, officers, fine ladies, boatmen, and the hundred other phases of Venetian life.

But I hear Espero's voice out on the broad water. Now I catch the sunlight on his white shirt and blue sash. He is standing erect, his whole body swaying with that long, graceful, sweeping stroke which is the envy of the young gondoliers and the despair of the old ; Espero, as you know, has been twice winner in the gondola races. He sees my signal, runs his bow close in, and the next instant we are swinging back up the Grand Canal, skirting the old boat-yard and the edge of the Piazzetta. A puff of smoke from the man-of-war ahead, and the roll of the sunset gun booms over the water. Before the echoes have fairly died away, a long, sinuous snake of employees — there are some seven thousand of them — crawls from out the arsenal gates, curves over the arsenal bridge, and heads up the Riva. On we go, abreast of the crowd, past the landing-wharf of the little steamers, past the rear porches of the queer caffès, past the

41

man-of-war, and a moment later are off the wine shop and my bridge. I part the curtains, and from my cushions can see the Duchess standing in the doorway, her arms akimbo, with all the awnings rolled back tight for the night. The bridge itself is smothered in a swarm of human flies, most of them bareheaded. As we sheer closer, one more ragged than the rest springs up and waves his hat. Then comes the refrain of that loveliest of all the Venetian boat songs, —

" Jammo, jammo neoppa, jammo ja."

It is Luigi, bidding me good-night.

THE PIAZZA OF SAN MARCO

THERE is but one Piazza in the world. There may be other splendid courts and squares, magnificent breathing spaces for the people, enriched by mosque and palace, bordered by wide-spreading trees, and adorned by noble statues. You know, of course, every slant of sunlight over the plaza of the Hippodrome, in Constantinople, with its slender twin needles of stone; you know the Puerta del Sol of Madrid, cooled by the splash of sunny fountains and alive with the rush of Spanish life; and you know, too, the royal Place de la Concorde, brilliant with the never-ending whirl of pleasure-loving Paris. Yes, you know and may love them all, and yet there is but one grand Piazza the world over; and that lies to-day in front of the church of San Marco.

It is difficult to account for this fascination. Sometimes you think it lurks in the exquisite taper of the Campanile. Sometimes you think the secret of its charm is hidden in masterly carvings, delicacy of arch, or refinement of

43

color. Sometimes the Piazza appeals to you only as the great open-air bric-à-brac shop of the universe, with its twin columns of stone stolen from the islands of the Archipelago ; its bronze horses, church doors, and altar-front wrested from Constantinople and the East; and its clusters of pillars torn from almost every heathen temple within reach of a Venetian galley.

When your eye becomes accustomed to the dazzling splendor of the surroundings, and you begin to analyze each grand feature of this Court of the Doges, you are even more enchanted and bewildered. San Marco itself no longer impresses you as a mere temple, with open portals and swinging doors, but as an exquisite jewel case of agate and ivory, resplendent in gems and precious stones. The clock tower, with its dial of blue and gold and its figures of bronze, is not, as of old, one of a row of buildings, but a priceless ornament that might adorn the palace of some King of the Giants ; while the Loggia of Sansovino could serve as a mantel for his banquet hall, and any one of the three bronze sockets of the flagstaffs, masterpieces of Leopardo, hold huge candles to light him to bed.

And behind all this beauty of form and charm of handicraft, how lurid the background of tradition, cruelty, and crime! Poor Doge Francesco Foscari, condemning his own innocent son Jacopo to exile and death, in that very room overlooking the square; the traitor Marino Faliero, beheaded on the Giant Stairs of the palace, his head bounding to the pavement below; the perfidies of the Council of Ten; the state murders, tortures, and banishments; the horrors of the prisons of the Piombi; the silent deathstroke of the unsigned denunciations dropped into the Bocca del Leone, — that fatal letter-box with its narrow mouth agape in the wall of stone, nightly filled with the secrets of the living, daily emptied of the secrets of the dead. All are here before you. The very stones their victims trod lie beneath your feet, their watersoaked cells but a step away.

As you pass between the twin columns of stone, — the pillars of Saint Theodore and of the Lion, — you shudder when you recall the fate of the brave Piedmontese, Carmagnola, a fate unfolding a chapter of cunning, ingratitude, and cruelty almost unparalleled in the history of Venice. You remember that for years this great hireling captain had led the armies of Venice and the Florentines against his former master, Philip of Milan; and that for years Venice had idolized the victorious warrior.

You recall the disastrous expedition against Cremona, a stronghold of Philip, and the subsequent anxiety of the Senate lest the sword of the great captain should be turned against Venice herself. You remember that one morning, as the story runs, a deputation entered the tent of the great captain and presented the confidence of the Senate and an invitation to return at once to Venice and receive the plaudits of the people. Attended by his lieutenant, Gonzaga, Carmagnola set out to obey. All through the plains of Lombardy, brilliant in their gardens of olive and vine, he was received with honor and welcome. At Mestre he was met by an escort of eight gentlemen in gorgeous apparel, special envoys dispatched by the Senate, who conducted him across the wide lagoon and down the Grand Canal, to this very spot on the Molo.

On landing from his sumptuous barge, the banks ringing with the shouts of the populace, he was led by his escort direct to the palace, and instantly thrust into an underground dungeon. Thirty days later, after a trial such as only the Senate of the period would tolerate, and gagged lest his indignant outcry might rebound in mutinous echoes, his head fell between the columns of San Marco.

There are other pages to which one could turn in this book of the past, pages rubricated in blood and black-lettered in crime. The book is opened here because this tragedy of Carmagnola recalls so clearly and vividly the methods and impulses of the times, and because, too, it occurred where all Venice could see, and where to-day you can conjure up for yourself the minutest details of the terrible outrage. Almost nothing of the scenery is changed. From where you stand between these fatal shafts, the same now as in the days of Carmagnola (even then two centuries old), there still hangs a balcony whence you could have caught the glance of that strong, mute warrior. Along the water's edge of this same Molo, where now the gondoliers ply their calling, and the *lasagnoni* lounge and gossip, stood the soldiers of the state drawn up in solid phalanx. Across the canal, by the margin of this same island of San Giorgio — before the present church was built — the people waited in masses, silently watching the group between those two stone posts that marked for them, and for all Venice, the doorway of hell. Above towered this same Campanile, all but its very top complete.

But you hurry away, crossing the square with a lingering look at this fatal spot, and en-

47

ter where all these and a hundred other trage-
dies were initiated, the Palace of the Doges. It
is useless to attempt a description of its wonderful details. If I should elaborate, it would
not help to give you a clearer idea of this marvel of the fifteenth century. To those who
know Venice, it will convey no new impression ;
to those who do not it might add only confusion
and error.

Give yourself up instead to the garrulous old
guide who assails you as you enter, and who,
for a few *lire*, makes a thousand years as one
day. It is he who will tell you of the beautiful
gate, the Porta della Carta of Bartolommeo Bon,
with its statues weather-stained and worn ; of
the famous Scala dei Giganti, built by Rizzo in
1485 ; of the two exquisitely moulded and
chased bronze wellheads of the court ; of the
golden stairs of Sansovino ; of the antechamber
of the Council of Ten ; of the great Sala di
Collegio, in which the foreign ambassadors
were received by the Doge ; of the superb senate chamber, the Sala del Senato ; of the costly
marbles and marvellous carvings ; of the ceilings of Titian, Tintoretto, and Veronese ; of the
secret passages, dungeons, and torture chambers.

But the greatest of all these marvels of the

Piazza still awaits you, the church of San Marco. Dismiss the old guide outside the beautiful gate and enter its doors alone ; here he would fail you.

If you come only to measure the mosaics, to value the swinging lamps, or to speculate over the uneven, half-worn pavement of the interior, enter its doors at any time, early morning or bright noonday, or whenever your practical, materialistic, nineteenth-century body would escape from the blaze of the sun outside. Or you can stay away altogether ; neither you nor the world will be the loser. But if you are the kind of man who loves all beautiful things, — it may be the sparkle of early dew upon the grass, the silence and rest of cool green woods, the gloom of the fading twilight, — or if your heart warms to the sombre tones of old tapestries, armor, and glass, and you touch with loving tenderness the vellum backs of old books, then enter when the glory of the setting sun sifts in and falls in shattered shafts of light on altar, roof, and wall. Go with noiseless step and uncovered head, and, finding some deep-shadowed seat or sheltered nook, open your heart and mind and soul to the story of its past, made doubly precious by the splendor of its present. As you sit there in the shadow, the

spell of its exquisite color will enchant you, —
color mellowing into harmonies you knew not of;
harmonies of old gold and porphyry reds; the
dull silver of dingy swinging lamps, with the
soft light of candles and the dreamy haze of dying incense; harmonies of rich brown carvings
and dark bronzes rubbed bright by a thousand
reverent hands.

The feeling which will steal over you will
not be one of religious humility, like that which
took possession of you in the Saint Sophia of
Constantinople. It will be more like the blind
idolatry of the pagan, for of all the temples of
the earth, this shrine of San Marco is the most
worthy of your devotion. Every turn of the
head will bring new marvels into relief, —
marvels of mosaic, glinting like beaten gold;
marvels of statue, crucifix, and lamp; marvels
of altars, resplendent in burnished silver and
flickering tapers; of alabaster columns merging
into the vistas; of sculptured saint and ceiling
of sheeted gold; of shadowy aisle and high uplifted cross.

Never have you seen any such interior. Hung
with the priceless fabrics and relics of the earth,
it is to you one moment a great mosque, studded
with jewels and rich with the wealth of the
East; then, as its color deepens, a vast tomb,

hollowed from out a huge, dark opal, in which lies buried some heroic soul, who in his day controlled the destinies of nations and of men. And now again, when the mystery of its light shimmers through windows covered with the dust of ages, there comes to this wondrous shrine of San Marco, small as it is, something of the breadth and beauty, the solitude and repose, of a summer night.

When the first hush and awe and sense of sublimity have passed away, you wander, like the other pilgrims, into the baptistery; or you move softly behind the altar, marvelling over each carving of wood and stone and bronze; or you descend to the crypt and stand by the stone sarcophagus that once held the bones of the good saint himself.

As you walk about these shadowy aisles, and into the dim recesses, some new devotee swings back a door, and a blaze of light streams in, and you awake to the life of to-day.

Yes, there is a present as well as a past. There is another Venice outside; a Venice of life and joyousness and stir. The sun is going down; the caffès under the arcades of the King's Palace and of the Procuratie Vecchie are filling up. There is hardly an empty table at Florian's. The pigeons, too, are coming home to roost, and are nestling under the eaves of the great buildings and settling on the carvings of San Marco. The flower girls, in gay costumes, are making shops of the marble benches next the Campanile, assorting roses and pinks, and arranging their *boutonnières* for the night's sale. The awnings which have hung all day between the columns of the arcades are drawn back, exposing the great line of shops fringing three sides of the square. Lights begin to flash ; first in the clusters of lamps illuminating the arcades, and then in the windows filled with exquisite bubble-blown Venetian glass, wood carvings, inlaid cabinets, cheap jewelry, gay-colored photographs and prints.

As the darkness falls, half a dozen men drag to the centre of the Piazza the segments of a great circular platform. This they surround with music-rests and a stand for the leader. Now the pavement of the Piazza itself begins filling up. Out from the Merceria, from under the clock tower, pours a steady stream of people merging in the crowds about the band stand. Another current flows in through the west entrance, under the Bocca di Piazza, and still another from under the Riva, rounding the Doges' Palace. At the Molo, just where poor Carmagnola stepped ashore, a group of officers — they are everywhere in Venice — land from a government barge. These are in full regalia, even to their white kid gloves, their swords dangling and ringing as they walk. They, too, make their way to the square and fill the seats around one of the tables at Florian's, bowing magnificently to the old Countess who sits just inside the door of the caffè itself, resplendent, as usual, in dyed wig and rose-colored veil. She is taking off her long, black, fingerless silk gloves, and ordering her customary spoonful of cognac and lump of sugar. Gustavo, the head waiter, listens as demurely as if he expected a bottle of Chablis at least, with the customary commission for Gustavo — but then Gustavo is the soul of politeness. Some evil-minded people say the Countess came in with the Austrians; others, more ungallant, date her advent about the days of the early Doges.

By this time you notice that the old French professor is in his customary place ; it is outside the caffè, in the corridor, on a leather-covered, cushioned seat against one of the high pillars. You never come to the Piazza without meeting him. He is as much a part of its history as the pigeons, and, like them, dines here at least once a day. He is a perfectly straight, pale, punctilious, and exquisitely deferential relic of a bygone time, whose only capital is his charming manner and his thorough knowledge of Venetian life. This combination rarely fails where so many strangers come and go ; and then, too, no one knows so well the intricacies of an Italian kitchen as Professor Croisac.

Sometimes on summer evenings he will move back a chair at your own table and insist upon dressing the salad. Long before his greeting, you catch sight of him gently edging his way through the throng, the seedy, straight-brimmed silk hat in his hand brushed with the greatest precision ; his almost threadbare frock coat buttoned snug around his waist, the collar and tails flowing loose, his one glove hanging limp. He is so erect, so gentle, so soft-voiced, so sincere, and so genuine, and for the hour so supremely happy, that you cannot divest yourself of the idea that he really is an old marquis, temporarily exiled from some far-away court, and to be treated with the greatest deference. When, with a little start of sudden surprise, he espies some dark-eyed matron in the group about him, rises to his feet and salutes her as if she were the Queen of Sheba, you are altogether sure of his noble rank. Then the old fellow regains his seat, poises his gold eyeglasses — a relic of better days — between his thumb and forefinger, holds them two inches from his nose, and consults the *menu* with the air of a connoisseur.

Before your coffee is served the whole Piazza is ablaze and literally packed with people. The tables around you stand quite out to the far-thest edge permitted. (These caffès have, so to speak, riparian rights — so much piazza seat-ing frontage, facing the high-water mark of the caffè itself.) The waiters can now hardly wedge their way through the crowd. The chairs are so densely occupied that you barely move your elbows. Next you is an Italian mother, full blown even to her delicate mus-tache, surrounded by a bevy of daughters, all in pretty hats and white or gay-colored dresses, chatting with a circle of still other officers. All over the square, where earlier in the day only a few stray pilgrims braved the heat, or a hun-gry pigeon wandered in search of a grain of corn, the personnel of this table is repeated, — mothers and officers and daughters, and daugh-ters and officers and mothers again.

Outside this mass, representing a *clientèle* possessing at least half a *lira* each — one can-not, of course, occupy a chair and spend less, and it is equally difficult to spend very much more — there moves in a solid mass the rest of the world : bareheaded girls, who have been

55

all day stringing beads in some hot courtyard;
old crones in rags from below the shipyards;
fishermen in from Chioggia ; sailors, stevedores,
and soldiers in their linen suits, besides sight-
seers and wayfarers from the four corners of the
earth.

If there were nothing else in Venice but the
night life of this grand Piazza, it would be worth
a pilgrimage half across the world to see. Empty
every café in the Boulevards; add all the *habitués* of the Volks-Gardens of Vienna, and all
those you remember at Berlin, Buda-Pesth, and
Florence ; pack them in one mass, and you
would not half fill the Piazza. Even if you did,
you could never bring together the same kinds
of people. Venice is the magnet that draws not
only the idler and the sight-seer, but those who
love her just because she is Venice, — painters,
students, architects, historians, musicians, every
soul who values the past and who finds here, as
nowhere else, the highest achievement of chisel,
brush, and trowel.

The painters come, of course — all kinds of
painters, for all kinds of subjects. Every morning, all over the canals and quays, you find
a new growth of white umbrellas, like mush-
rooms, sprung up in the night. Since the days
of Canaletto these men have painted and re-

painted these same stretches of water, palace, and sky. Once under the spell of her presence, they are never again free from the fascinations of this Mistress of the Adriatic. Many of the older men are long since dead and forgotten, but the work of those of to-day you know, — Ziem first, nearly all his life a worshipper of the wall of the Public Garden; and Rico and Ruskin and Whistler. Their names are legion. They have all had a corner at Florian's. No matter what their nationality or specialty, they speak the common language of the brush. Old Professor Croisac knows them all. He has just risen again to salute Marks, a painter of sunrises, who has never yet recovered from his first thrill of delight when early one morning his gondolier rowed him down the lagoon and made fast to a cluster of spiles off the Public Garden. When the sun rose behind the sycamores and threw a flood of gold across the sleeping city, and flashed upon the sails of the fishing-boats drifting up from the Lido, Marks lost his heart. He is still tied up every summer to that same cluster of spiles, painting the glory of the morning sky and the drifting boats. He will never want to paint anything else. He will not listen to you when you tell him of the sunsets up the Giudecca, or the soft pearly light of the dawn silvering the Salute, or the picturesque life of the fisher-folk of Malamocco.

"My dear boy," he breaks out, "get up to-morrow morning at five and come down to the Garden, and just see one sunrise — only one. We had a lemon-yellow and pale emerald sky this morning, with dabs of rose leaves, that would have paralyzed you."

Do not laugh at the painter's enthusiasm. This white goddess of the sea has a thousand lovers, and like all other lovers the world over, each one believes that he alone holds the key to her heart.

IN AN OLD GARDEN

YOU think, perhaps, there are no gardens in Venice; that it is all a sweep of palace front and shimmering sea; that save for the oleanders bursting into bloom near the Iron Bridge, and the great trees of the Public Garden shading the flower-bordered walks, there are no half-neglected tangles where rose and vine run riot; where the plash of the fountain is heard in the stillness of the night, and tall cedars cast their black shadows at noonday.

Really, if you but knew it, almost every palace hides a garden nestling beneath its balconies, and every high wall hems in a wealth of green, studded with broken statues, quaint arbors festooned with purple grapes, and white walks bordered by ancient box, — while every roof that reaches to a window is made a hanging garden of potted plants and swinging vines.

Step from your gondola into some open archway. A door beyond leads you to a court paved with marble flags and centred by a well with carved marble curb, yellow-stained with age. Cross this wide court, pass a swinging iron gate, and you stand under rose-covered bowers, where in the olden time gay gallants touched their lutes and fair ladies listened to oft-told tales of love.

And not only behind the palaces facing the Grand Canal, but along the Zattere beyond San Rosario, away down the Giudecca, and by the borders of the lagoon, will you find gay oleanders flaunting red blossoms, and ivy and myrtle hanging in black-green bunches over crumbling walls.

In one of these hidden nooks, these abandoned cloisters of shaded walk and over-bending blossom, I once spent an autumn afternoon with my old friend, the Professor, — "Professor of Modern Languages and Ancient Legends," as some of the more flippant of the *habitués* of Florian's were wont to style him. The old Frenchman had justly earned this title. He had not only made every tradition and fable of Venice his own, often puzzling and charming the Venetians themselves with his intimate knowledge of the many romances of their past, but he could tell most wonderful tales of the gorgeous fêtes of the seventeenth century, the social life of the nobility, their escapades, intrigues, and scandals.

If some fair Venetian had loved not wisely but too well, and, clinging to brave Lorenzo's neck, had slipped down a rope ladder into a closely curtained, muffled-oared gondola, and so over the lagoon to Mestre, the old Frenchman could not only point out to you the very balcony, provided it were a palace balcony and not a fisherman's window, — he despised the *bourgeoisie,* — but he could give you every feature of the escapade, from the moment the terror-stricken duenna missed her charge to that of the benediction of the priest in the shadowed isle. So, when upon the evening preceding this particular day, I accepted the Professor's invitation to breakfast, I had before me not only his hospitality, frugal as it might be, but the possibility of drawing upon his still more delightful fund of anecdote and reminiscence.

Neither the day nor the hour had been definitely set. The invitation, I afterwards discovered, was but one of the many he was constantly giving to his numerous friends and haphazard acquaintances, evincing by its perfect genuineness his own innate kindness and his hearty appreciation of the many similar courtesies he was daily receiving at their hands.

Indeed, to a man so delicately adjusted as the Professor and so entirely poor, it was the only way he could balance, in his own mind, many long-running accounts of coffee for two at the Calcina, with a fish and a fruit salad, the last a specialty of the Professor's — the oil, melons, and cucumbers being always provided by his host — or a dish of *risotto*, with kidneys and the like, at the Bauer-Grünwald.

Nobody ever accepted these invitations seriously, that is, no one who knew the Professor at all well. In fact, there was a general impression existing among the many frequenters of Florian's and the Quadri that the Professor's hour and place of breakfasting were very like the birds', — whenever the unlucky worm was found, and wherever the accident happened to occur. When I asked Marks for the old fellow's address, which rather necessary item I remembered later had also been omitted by the Professor, he replied, " Oh, somewhere down the Riva," and dropped the subject as too unimportant for further mental effort.

All these various eccentricities of my prospective host, however, were at the time unknown to me. He had cordially invited me to breakfast, — " to-morrow, or any day you are near my apartments, I would be so charmed," etc.

I had as graciously accepted, and it would have been unpardonable indifference, I felt sure, not to have continued the inquiries until my hand touched his latch-string.

The clue was a slight one. I had met him once, leaning over the side of the bridge below Danieli's, the Ponte del Sepolcro, looking wistfully out to sea, and was greeted with the remark that he had that moment left his apartments, and only lingered on the bridge to watch the play of silvery light on the lagoon, the September skies were so enchanting. So on this particular morning I began inspecting the bellpulls of all the doorways, making inquiry at the several caffès and shops. Then I remembered the apothecary, down one step from the sidewalk, in the Via Garibaldi — a rather shabby continuation of the Riva — and nearly a mile below the more prosperous quarter where the Professor had waved his hand, the morning I met him on the bridge.

" The Signor Croisac — the old Frenchman ? Upstairs, next door."

He was as delightful as ever in his greetings ; started a little when I reminded him of his invitation, but begged me to come in and sit down, and with great courtesy pointed out the view of the garden below, and the sweep and

63

glory of the lagoon. Then he excused himself, adjusted his hat, picked up a basket, and gently closed the door.

The room, upon closer inspection, was neither dreary nor uninviting. It had a sort of annex, or enlarged closet, with a drawn curtain partly concealing a bed, a row of books lining one wall, a table littered with papers, a smaller one containing a copper coffee-pot and a scant assortment of china, some old chairs, and a disembowelled lounge that had doubtless lost heart in middle life and committed hari-kari. There were also a few prints and photographs, a corner of the Parthenon, a mezzo of Napoleon in his cocked hat, and an etching or two, besides a miniature reduction of the Dying Gladiator, which he used as a paper-weight. All the windows of this modest apartment were filled with plants, growing in all kinds of pots and boxes, broken pitchers, cracked dishes — even half of a Chianti flask. These, like their guardian, ignored their surroundings and furnishings, and flamed away as joyously in the summer sun as if they had been nurtured in the choicest of majolica.

He was back before I had completed my inventory, thanking me again and again for my extreme kindness in coming, all the while unwrapping the Gorgonzola, and flecking off with a fork the shreds of paper that still clung to its edges. The morsel was then laid upon a broad leaf picked at the window, and finally upon a plate covered by a napkin so that the flies should not taste it first. This, with a simple salad, a pot of coffee and some rolls, a siphon of seltzer and a little raspberry juice in a glass, — "so much fresher than wine these hot mornings," he said, — constituted the entire repast.

But there was no apology offered with the serving. Poor as he was, he had that exquisite tact which avoided burdening his guest even with his economies. He had offered me all his slender purse could afford. Indeed, the cheese had quite overstrained it.

When he had drawn a cigarette from my case, — it was delightful to see him do this, and always reminded me of a young girl picking bonbons from a box, it was so daintily done, — the talk drifted into a discussion of the glories of the old days and of the welfare of Italy under the present government. I made a point of expressing my deep admiration for the good King Humbert and his gracious queen. The Professor merely waved his hand, adding, —

"Yes, a good man and a noble lady, worthy

65

successors of the old régime ! " Then, with a
certain air, " I have known, professionally, very
many of these great families. A most charming, delightful society ! The women so exquisite, with such wealth of hair and eyes, and so
gentilles, — always of the *Beau Monde !* And
their traditions and legends, so full of romance
and mystery ! The palaces too ! Think of the
grand staircase of the Foscari,the entrance to the
Barbaro, and the superb ceilings of the Albrezzi !
Then their great gardens and vine orchards !
There is nothing like them. Do you happen to
know the old garden on the Giudecca, where
lived the beautiful Contessa Alberoni ? No ?
And you never heard the romantic story of her
life, her disappearance, and its dramatic ending ? "

I shook my head. The Professor, to my delight, was now fairly in the saddle ; the best
part of the breakfast was to come.

"My dear friend ! One of the most curious
of all the stories of Venice ! I know intimately
many of her descendants, and I know, too, the
old gardener who still cares for what is left of
the garden. It has long since passed out of the
hands of the family.

"Let me light another cigarette before I tell
you," said the Professor, crossing the room,

"and just another drop of seltzer," filling my glass.

"Is it to be a true story?" I asked.

"*Mon cher ami!* absolutely so. Would you care to see the garden itself, where it all occurred, or will you take my word for it? No, not until you sit under the arbors and lean over the very balcony where the lovers sat. Come, is your gondola here? Under the window?" pushing aside the flowers. "Which is your gondolier? The one in blue with the white *tenda* over his boat? Yes, sound asleep like all the rest of them!"

Here the old gentleman picked up his silk hat, passed his hand once or twice around its well-brushed surface, discarded it for a white straw with a narrow black band, adjusted his cravat in a broken mirror that hung near the door, gave an extra twist to his gray mustache, and preceded me downstairs and out into the blinding light of a summer day.

Several members of the Open-Air Club were hanging over the bridge as we passed, — Luigi flat on his face and sound asleep in the shadow of the side wall, and Vittorio sprawled out on the polished rail above. Those who were awake touched their hats respectfully to the old fellow as he crossed the bridge, he returning their salutations quite as a distinguished earl would those of his tenants. Vittorio, when he caught my eye, sprang down and ran ahead to rouse Espero, and then back for Luigi, who awoke with a dazed look on his face, only regaining consciousness in time to wave his hat to me when we were clear of the quay, the others standing in a row enjoying his discomfiture.

"This garden," continued the Professor, settling himself on the cushions and drawing the curtains so that he could keep the view toward San Giorgio and still shut out the dazzling light, "is now, of course, only a ghost of its former self. The château is half in ruins, and one part is inhabited by fishermen, who dry their nets in the grape arbors and stow their fish baskets in the porticoes. Many of the fruit-trees, however, still exist, as do many of the vines, and so my old friend Angelo, the gardener, makes a scanty living for himself and his pretty daughter, by supplying the fruit-stands in the autumn and raising lettuce and melons in the spring and summer. The ground itself, like most of the land along the east side of the islands of the Giudecca, is valueless, and everything is falling into ruin."

We were rounding the Dogana, Espero bending lustily to his oar as we shot past the wood-boats anchored in the stream. The Professor talked on, pointing out the palace where Pierre, the French adventurer, lived during the Spanish conspiracy, and the very side door in the old building, once a convent, from which an Englishman in the old days had stolen a nun who loved him, and spirited her off to another quaint nook in this same Giudecca, returning her to her cell every morning before daybreak.

" Ah, those were the times to live in! Then a *soldo* was as large as a *lira*. Then a woman loved you for yourself, not for what you gave her. Then your gondolier kept your secrets, and the keel of your boat left no trace behind. Then your family crest meant something more than the name-plate on your door, upon which to nail a tax levy."

The old man had evidently forgotten his history, but I did not check him. It was his buoyant enthusiasm that always charmed me most.

As Espero passed under Ponte Lungo, the wooden bridge leading to the Fondamenta della Pallada, the Professor waved his hand to the right, and we floated out into the lagoon and stopped at an old water-gate, its doors weather-stained and broken, over which hung a mass of tangled vines.

69

"The garden of the Contessa," said the Professor, his face aglow with the expectancy of my pleasure.

It was like a dozen other water-gates I had seen, except that no gratings were open and the surrounding wall was unusually high. Once inside, however, with the gate swung to on its rusty hinges, you felt instantly that the world had been shut away forever. Here were long arbors bordered by ancient box, with arching roofs of purple grapes. Against the high walls stood fragments of statues, some headless, some with broken arms or battered faces. Near the centre of the great quadrangle was a sunken basin, covered with mould, and green with the scum of stagnant water. In the once well-regulated garden beds the roses bloomed gayly, climbing over pedestal and statue, while the trumpet-flower and scarlet-creeper flaunted their colors high upon the crumbling walls overlooking the lagoon. At one end of this tangled waste rose the remains of a once noble château or summer home, built of stone in the classic style of architecture, the pediment of the porch supported by a row of white marble columns. Leaning against these columns stood old fish baskets, used for the storing of live fish, while over the ruined arbors hung in great festoons the nets of a neighboring fisherman, who reserved this larger space for drying and mending his seines.

It was a ruin, and yet not a hopeless one. You could see that each year the flowers struggled into life again; that the old black cypresses, once trimmed into quaint designs, had still determined to live on, even without the care of their arboreal barber; that really only the pruning knife and spade were needed to bring back the garden to its former beauty. And the solitude was there too, the sense of utter isolation, as if the outside world were across the sea, whither nor eye nor voice could follow.

Old Angelo and his pretty daughter — a pure type of the Venetian girl of to-day, as she stood expectantly with folded arms — met us at the gate, and led the way to a sort of summer-house, so thickly covered with matted vines that the sun only filtered through and fell in drops of gold, spattering the ground below. Here, incrusted with green mould, was a marble table of exquisite design, its circular top supported by a tripod with lions' feet.

Angelo evidently knew my companion and his ways, for in a few moments the girl returned, bringing a basket of grapes, some figs, and a flask of wine. The Professor thanked her, and then, dismissing her with one of his gentle hand-waves and brushing the fallen leaves from the stone bench with his handkerchief, sat down.

"And now, right here," said the old fellow, placing his straw hat upon the seat beside him, his gray hair glistening in the soft light, "right here, where she loved and died, I will tell you the story of the Contessa Alberoni.

"This most divine of women once lived in a grand old palace above the Rialto. She belonged to a noble family of Florence, whose ancestors fought with Philip, before the Campanile was finished. All over Italy she was known as the most beautiful woman of her day, and that, let me tell you, at a time when to be counted as beautiful in Venice was to be beautiful the world over. She was a woman," — here the Professor rested his head on the marble seat and half closed his eyes, as if he were recalling the vision of loveliness from out his own past, — "well, one of those ideal women, with fathomless eyes and rounded white arms and throat; a Catherine Cornaro type, of superb carriage and presence. Titian would have lost his heart over the torrent of gold that fell in masses about her shapely head, and Canova

might have exhausted all his skill upon the outlines of her form.

"In the beginning of her womanhood, when
yet barely sixteen, she had married, at her father's bidding, a decrepit Italian count nearly
thrice her age, who, in profound consideration
of her sacrifice, died in a becoming manner
within a few years of their marriage, leaving
her his titles and estates. For ten years of her
wedded life and after, she lived away off in the
secluded villa of Valdagna, a small town nestling among the foothills of the Alps. Then,
suddenly awakening to the power of her wonderful beauty, she took possession of the great
palace on the Grand Canal above the Rialto.
You can see it any day ; and save that some
of the spindles in the exquisite rose-marble balconies are broken and the façade blackened and
weather-stained, the exterior is quite as it appeared in her time. The interior, however, owing to the obliteration of this noble family and
the consequent decay of its vast estates, is almost a ruin. Every piece of furniture and all
the gorgeous hangings are gone ; together with
the mantels, and the superb well-curb in the
court below. Tell Espero to take you there
some day. You will not only find the grand entrance blocked with wine casks, but my lady's

boudoir plastered over with cheap green paper and rented as cheaper lodgings to still cheaper tenants. Bah ! "

Then the Professor, dropping easily and gracefully into a style of delivery as stilted as if he were remembering the very words of some old chronicle, told me how she had lived in this grand palace during the years of her splendor, the pride and delight of all who came under her magic spell, as easily Queen of Venice as Venice was Queen of the Sea. How at thirty, then in the full radiance of her beauty, beloved and besought by every hand that could touch her own, painters vied with each other in matching the tints of her marvellous skin ; sculptors begged for models of her feet to grace their masterpieces ; poets sang her praises, and the first musicians of Italy wrote the songs that her lovers poured out beneath her windows. How there had come a night when suddenly the whole course of her life was changed, — the night of a great ball given at one of the old palaces on the Grand Canal, the festivities ending with a pageant that revived the sumptuous days of the Republic, in which the Contessa herself was to take part.

When the long-expected hour arrived, she was seen to step into her gondola, attired in a dress of the period, a marvel of velvet and cloth-of-gold. Then she disappeared as completely from human sight as if the waters of the canal had closed over her forever.

For days all investigation proved fruitless. The only definite clue came from her gondolier, who said that soon after the gondola had left the steps of her palace, the Contessa ordered him to return home at once; that on reaching the landing she covered her face with her veil and reëntered the palace. Later it was whispered that for many weeks she had not left her apartments. Then she sent for her father confessor, and at a secret interview announced her decision never again to appear to the world.

At this point of the story the Professor had risen from his seat and poured half the flagon into his glass. He was evidently as much absorbed in the recital as if it had all happened yesterday. I could see, too, that it appealed to those quaint, romantic views of life which, for all their absurdities, endeared the old fellow to every one who knew him.

"For a year," he continued, "this seclusion was maintained; no one saw the Contessa, not even her own servants. Her meals were served behind a screen. Of course all Venice was agog. Every possible solution of so strange and unexpected a seclusion was suggested and discussed.

"In the beginning of the following winter vague rumors reached the good father's ears. One morning he left his devotions, and, waylaying her duenna outside the palace garden, pressed his rosary into her hands and said, 'Take this to the Contessa.'" Here the Professor became very dramatic, holding out his hand with a quick gesture, as if it clasped the rosary. "'Tell her that to-night, when San Giorgio strikes twelve, I shall be at the outer gate of the palace and must be admitted.'"

Then pacing up and down the narrow arbor, his face flushed, his eyes glistening, the old fellow told the rest of the story. "When," said he, "the hour arrived, the heavy grated door, the same through which you can now see the wine casks, was cautiously opened. A moment later the priest was ushered into a dimly lighted room, luxuriously furnished, and screened at one end by a silken curtain, behind which sat the Contessa. She listened while he told her how all Venice was outraged at her conduct, many hearts being grieved and many tongues dropping foul slander. He remonstrated with her about the life she was leading, condemning its selfishness and threatening the severest discipline. But neither threats nor the voice of slander intimidated the Contessa. She steadfastly avowed that her life had been blameless, and despite the earnest appeals of the priest persisted in the determination to live the rest of her days in quiet and seclusion. The most he was able to effect was a promise that within a month she would open the doors of her palace for one more great ball. Her friends would then be reassured and her enemies silenced.

" The records show that no such festival had been seen in Venice for many years. The palace was a blaze of light. So great was the crush of gondolas bringing their beauteous freight of richly dressed Venetians, that the traffic of the canal was obstructed for hours. Ten o'clock came, eleven, and still there was no Contessa to welcome her guests. Strange stories were set afloat. It was whispered that a sudden illness had overtaken her. Then, as the hours wore on, the terrible rumor gained credence that she had been murdered by her servants, and that the report of her illness was only a cloak to conceal their crime.

" While the excitement was at its height, a man, in the costume of a herald, appeared in the great salon and announced the arrival of the hostess. As the hour struck twelve a curtain

was drawn at the farther end of the room, re-
vealing the Contessa seated upon a dais, superbly attired in velvet and lace, and brilliant
with jewels. When the hum and wonder of the
surprise had ceased, she arose, stood like a queen
receiving the homage of her subjects, and, welcoming her guests to her palace, bade them
dance on until the sun rose over the Lido. Then
the curtains were drawn, and so ended the last
sight of the Contessa in Venice. Her palace was
never opened again. Later she disappeared completely, and the spiders spun their webs across
the threshold.

"Years afterward, a man repairing a high
chimney on a roof overlooking this very garden — the chimney can still be seen from the
far corner below the landing — saw entering the
arbor a noble lady, leaning upon the arm of a
distinguished-looking man of about her own
age. In the lady he recognized the Contessa.

"Little by little the story came out. It
appeared that immediately after the ball she
had moved to this château, a part of her own
estates, which had been quietly fitted up and
restored. It was then remembered that soon
after the château had been finished, a certain
marquis, well known in France, who had adored
the Contessa for years, and was really the

only man she ever loved, had disappeared from Paris. He was traced at the time to Milan and Genoa, and finally to Venice. There all trace of him was lost. Such disappearances were not uncommon in those days, and it was often safer even for one's relatives to shrug their shoulders and pass on. Further confirmation came from the gondolier, who had landed him the night of his arrival at the water-gate of this garden, — just where we landed an hour ago, — and who, on hearing of his supposed murder, had kept silent upon his share in the suspected crime. Inquiries conducted by the state corroborated these facts.

"Look around you, *mon ami*," exclaimed the Professor suddenly. "Underneath this very arbor have they sat for hours, and in the window of that crumbling balcony have they listened to the low sound of each other's voices in the still twilight, the world shut out, the vine-covered wall their only horizon. Here, as the years passed unheeded, they dreamed their lives away. L'amour, l'amour, vous êtes tout puissant!"

The Professor stopped, turned as if in pain, and rested his head on his arm. For some moments neither of us spoke. Was the romance to which I had listened only the romance of the

Contessa, or had he unconsciously woven into its meshes some of the silken threads of his own past? When he raised his head I said, "But, Professor, you have not told me the secret she kept from the priest. Why did she shut herself up? What was it that altered the whole course of her life?"

"Did I not tell you? Then listen. She had overheard her gondolier say, as she stepped into her gondola on the fatal night of the great fête at the Foscari, 'The Contessa is growing old; she is no longer as beautiful as she was.'"

I looked at the old fellow to see if he were really in earnest, and throwing back my head, laughed heartily. For the first time in all my intercourse with him I saw the angry color mount to his cheeks.

He turned quickly, looked at me in astonishment, as if unable to believe his ears, and said sharply, knitting his brows, "Why do you laugh?"

"It seems so absurd," I replied. "What did she expect, — to be always a goddess?"

"Ah, there you go!" he burst out again, with flashing eyes. "That is just like a cold-blooded materialist. I hate your modern Shylock, who can see a pound of flesh cut from a human heart with no care for the hot blood that follows. Have you no sympathy deep down in your soul for a woman when she realizes for the first time that her hold on the world is slipping? Can you not understand the agony of the awakening from a long dream of security and supremacy, when she finds that others are taking her place? The daily watching for the loss of color, the fulness of the waist, the pencilling of care-lines about the eyes? We men have bodily force and mental vigor, and sometimes lifelong integrity, to commend us, and as we grow older and the first two fail, the last serves us best of all; but what has a woman like the Contessa left? I am not talking of an ordinary woman, nor of all the good daughters, good wives, and good mothers in the world. You expect in such women the graces of virtue, duty, and resignation. I am talking of a superb creature whom the good God created just to show the world what the angels looked like. I insist that before you laugh you must put yourself in the place of this noble Contessa whom all Venice adored, whose reign for fifteen years had been supreme, whose beauty was to her something tangible, — a weapon, a force, an atmosphere. She had all the other charms that adorned the women of her day, good humor, a rich mind, charity, and wit, but so had a hundred other Venetians of her class. I insist that before censuring her, you enter the salon and watch with her the faces of her guests, noting her eagerness to detect the first glance of delight or disappointment, and her joy or chagrin as she reads the verdict in their eyes. Can you not realize that in a beauty such as hers there is an essence, a spirit, a something divine and ethereal ? A something like the bloom on these grapes, adding the exquisite to their lusciousness ; like the pure color of the diamond, intensifying its flash ? A something that, in addition to all her other qualities, makes a woman transcendent and should make her immortal ? We men long for this divine quality, adore it, go mad over it ; and yet when it has faded, with an inconstancy and neglect which to me is one of the enigmas of human nature, we shrug our shoulders, laugh, and pass on. Believe me, *mon ami*, when that gondolier confirmed the looking-glass of the Contessa, his words fell upon her ears like earth upon her coffin.''

If the Professor's emotion at the close of the story was a surprise to me, this frenzied outburst, illogical and quixotic as it seemed, was equally unexpected. I could hardly realize that this torrent of fiery passion and pent-up energy had burst from the frail, plain little body before me. Again and again, as I looked at him, the thought ran through my mind, Whom had he loved like that ? What had come between himself and his own Contessa ? Why was this man an exile, — this cheery, precise, ever courteous, dignified old thoroughbred, with his dry, crackling exterior, and his volcano of a heart beneath? Or was it Venice, with her wealth of traditions, — traditions he had made his own, — that had turned his head ?

Long after the Professor left the garden, I sat looking about me, noting the broken walls overhung with matted vines, and the little lizards darting in and out. Then I strolled on and entered the doorway of the old château, and looked long and steadily at the ruined balcony, half buried in a tangle of roses, the shadows of their waving blossoms splashing the weather-stained marble ; and thence to the apartment above, where these same blossoms thrust themselves far into its gloom, as if they, too, would search for the vision of loveliness that had vanished. Then I wandered into an alcove sheltering the remains of an altar and font, — the very chapel, no doubt, where the good priest had married her ; on through the unkept walks bordered on each side by rows of ancient box, with here and there a gap where the sharp tooth of some winter more cruel than the rest had bitten deep, and so out again into the open garden, where I sat down under a great tree that sheltered the head of a Madonna built into the wall, — the work of Canova, the Professor had told me.

Despite my own convictions, I seem to feel the presence of these spirits of the past that the Professor, in his simple, earnest way, had conjured up before me, and to see on every hand evidences of their long life of happiness. The ruined balcony, with its matted rose vines, had now a deeper meaning. How often had the beautiful Venetian leaned over this same iron grating and watched her lover in the garden below ! On how many nights, made glorious by the radiance of an Italian moon, had they listened to the soft music of passing gondolas beyond the garden walls ?

The whole romance, in spite of its improbability and my thoughtless laughter, had affected me deeply. Why, I could not tell. Perhaps it was the Professor's enthusiasm ; perhaps his reverence for the beauty of woman, as well as for the Contessa herself. Perhaps he had really been recalling a chapter out of his own past,

before exile and poverty had made him a wan-
derer and a dreamer. Perhaps ! — Yes, perhaps
it was the thought of the long, quiet life of the
Contessa with her lover in this garden.

AMONG THE FISHERMEN

I KNOW best the fishing quarter of Ponte Lungo and the district near by, from the wooden bridge to the lagoon, with the side canal running along the Fondamenta della Pallada. This to me is not only the most picturesque quarter of Venice, but quite the most picturesque spot I know in Europe, except, perhaps, Scutari on the Golden Horn.

This quality of the picturesque saturates Venice. You find it in her stately structures; in her spacious Piazza, with its noble Campanile, clock tower, and façade of San Marco; in her tapering towers, deep - wrought bronze, and creamy marble; in her cluster of butterfly sails on far-off, wide horizons; in her opalescent dawns, flaming sunsets, and star-lit summer nights. You find it in the gatherings about her countless bridges spanning dark waterways; in the ever-changing color of crowded markets; in lazy gardens lolling over broken walls; in twisted canals, quaint doorways, and soggy, ooze-covered landing-steps. You find it, too, in many a dingy palace, — many a lop-sided old palace, with door jambs and windows askew, with lintels craning their heads over the edge, ready to plunge headlong into the canal below.

The little devils of rot and decay, deep down in the water, are at the bottom of all this settling and toppling of jamb and lintel. They are really the guardians of the picturesque.

Search any façade in Venice, from flow-line to cornice, and you cannot find two lines plumb or parallel. This is because these imps of destruction have helped the teredo to munch and gnaw and bore, undermining foundation pile, grillage, and bed-stone. If you listen some day over the side of your gondola, you will hear one of these old piles creak and groan as he sags and settles, and then up comes a bubble, as if all the fiends below had broken into a laugh at their triumph.

This change goes on everywhere. No sooner does some inhabitant of the earth build a monstrosity of right-angled triangles, than the little imps set to work. They know that Mother Nature detests a straight line, and so they summon all the fairy forces of sun, wind, and frost, to break and bend and twist, while they scuttle and bore and dig, until some fine morning after a siege of many years, you stumble upon their victim. The Doge who built it would shake his head in despair, but you forgive the tireless little devils — they have made it so delightfully picturesque.

To be exact, there are really fewer straight lines in Venice than in any other place in Europe. This is because all the islands are spiked full of rotting piles, holding up every structure within their limits. The constant settling of these wooden supports has dropped the Campanile nearly a foot out of plumb on the eastern façade, threatened the destruction of the southwest corner of the Doges' Palace, rolled the exquisite mosaic pavement of San Marco into waves of stone, and almost toppled into the canal many a church tower and garden wall.

Then, again, there are localities about Venice where it seems that every other quality except that of the picturesque has long since been annihilated. You feel it especially in the narrow side canal of the Public Garden, in the region back of the Rialto, through the Fruit Market, and in the narrow streets beyond, — so narrow that you can touch both sides in passing, the very houses leaning over like gossiping old crones, their foreheads almost touching. You feel it too in the gardens along the Giudecca, with their long arbors and tangled masses of

climbing roses ; in the interiors of many court-
yards along the Grand Canal, with *pozzo* and
surrounding pillars supporting the rooms above ;
in the ship and gondola repair-yards of the lagoons and San Trovaso, and more than all in
the fishing quarters, the one beyond Ponte Lungo
and those near the Arsenal, out towards San
Pietro di Castello.

This district of Ponte Lungo — the one I love
most — lies across the Giudecca, on the "Island of the Giudecca," as it is called, and is
really an outskirt, or rather a suburb of the
Great City. There are no grand palaces here.
Sometimes, tucked away in a garden, you will
find an old château, such as the Contessa occupied; and between the bridge and the *fondamenta* there is a row of great buildings, bris-
tling with giant chimneys, that might once have
been warehouses loaded with the wealth of the
East, but which are now stuffed full of old sails,
snarled seines, great fish baskets, oars, fishermen, fisher-wives, fisher-children, rags, old
clothes, bits of carpet, and gay, blossoming
plants in nondescript pots. I may be wrong
about these old houses being *stuffed full* of
these several different kinds of material, from
their damp basement floors to the fourth-story
garrets under baking red tiles ; but they cer-

tainly look so, for all these things, including the fisher-folk themselves, are either hanging out or thrust out of window, balcony, or doorway, thus proving conclusively the absurdity of there being even standing room inside.

Fronting the doors of these buildings are little rickety platforms of soggy planks, and running out from them, foot-walks of a single board, propped up out of the wet on poles, leading to fishing-smacks with sails of orange and red, the decks lumbered with a miscellaneous lot of fishing-gear and unassorted sea-truck, — buckets, seines, booms, dip-nets, and the like.

Aboard these boats the fishermen are busily engaged in scrubbing the sides and rails, and emptying the catch of the morning into their great wicker baskets, which either float in the water or are held up on poles by long strings of stout twine.

All about are more boats, big and little : row-boats ; storage-boats piled high with empty crab baskets, or surrounded with a circle of other baskets moored to cords and supported by a frame of hop-poles, filled with fish or crabs ; *barche* from across the lagoon, laden with green melons ; or lighters on their way to the Dogana from the steamers anchored behind the Giudecca.

Beyond and under the little bridge that leads up the Pallada, the houses are smaller and only flank one side of the narrow canal. On the other side, once an old garden, there is now a long, rambling wall, with here and there an opening, through which, to your surprise, you catch the drooping figure of a poor, forlorn mule, condemned for some crime of his ancestors to go round and round in a treadmill, grinding refuse brick. Along the quay or *fondamenta* of this narrow canal, always shady after ten o'clock, lie sprawled the younger members of these tenements, — the children, bareheaded, barefooted, and most of them barebacked ; while their mothers and sisters choke up the doorways, stringing beads, making lace, sitting in bunches listening to a story by some old crone, or breaking out into song, the whole neighborhood joining in the chorus.

Up at the farther end of the Pallada and under another wooden bridge, where two slips of canals meet, there is a corner that has added more sketches to my portfolio than any single spot in Venice. An old fisherman lives here, perhaps a dozen old fishermen ; they come and go all the time. There is a gate with a broken door, and a neglected garden trampled down by many feet, a half-ruined wall with fig-trees and

oleanders peeping over from the garden next
door, a row of ragged, straggling trees lining
the water's edge, and more big fish and crab
baskets scattered all about, — baskets big as
feather beds, — and festoons of nets hung to
the branches of the trees or thrown over the
patched-up fences, — every conceivable and in-
conceivable kind of fishing plunder that could
litter up the premises of a *pescatore* of the lagoon. In and out of all this débris swarm the
children, playing baby-house in the big baskets,
asleep under the overturned boat with the new
patch on her bottom, or leaning over the wall
catching little crabs that go nibbling along a
few inches below the water-line.

In this picturesque spot, within biscuit-throw
of this very corner, I have some very intimate
and charming friends — little Amelia, the child
model, and young Antonio, who is determined
to be a gondolier when he grows up, and who,
perhaps, could earn a better living by posing
for some sculptor as a Greek god. Then, too,
there is his mother, the Signora Marcelli, who
sometimes reminds me of my other old friend,
the " Grand Duchess of the Riva," who keeps
the caffè near the Ponte Veneta Marina.

The Signora Marcelli, however, lacks most of
the endearing qualities of the Duchess; one

in particular, — a soft, musical voice. If the signora is in temporary want of the services of one of her brood of children, it never occurs to her, no matter where she may be, to send another member of the household in search of the missing child ; she simply throws back her head, fills her lungs, and begins a *crescendo* which terminates in a *fortissimo*, so shrill and far-reaching that it could call her offspring back from the dead. Should her husband, the Signor Marcelli, come in some wet morning late from the lagoon, — say at nine o'clock, instead of an hour after daylight, — the signora begins on her *crescendo* when she first catches sight of his boat slowly poled along the canal. Thereupon the signora fills the surrounding air with certain details of her family life, including her present attitude of mind toward the signore, and with such volume and vim that you think she fully intends breaking every bone under his tarpaulins when he lands, — and she is quite able physically to do it, — until you further notice that it makes about as much impression upon the signore as the rain upon his oilskins. It makes still less on his neighbors, who have listened to similar outbursts for years, and have come to regard them quite as they would the announcement by one of the signora's hens

93

that she had just laid an egg, — an event of too much importance to be passed over in silence.

When the Signor Marcelli arrives off the little wooden landing-ladder facing his house, and, putting things shipshape about the boat, enters his doorway, thrashing the water from his tarpaulin hat as he walks, the signora, from sheer loss of breath, subsides long enough to overhaul a unique collection of dry clothing hanging to the rafters, from which she selects a coat patched like Joseph's of old, with trousers to match. These she carries to the signore, who puts them on in dead silence, reappearing in a few moments barefooted but dry, a red worsted cap on his head, and a short pipe in his mouth. Then he drags up a chair, and, still silent as a graven image, — he has not yet spoken a word, — continues smoking, looking furtively up at the sky, or leaning over listlessly and watching the chickens that gather about his feet. Now and again he picks up a rooster or strokes a hen as he would a kitten. Nothing more.

Only then does the signora subside, bringing out a fragment of *polenta* and a pot of coffee, which the fisherman divides with his chickens, the greedy ones jumping on his knees. I feel assured that it is neither discretion nor domestic

tact, nor even uncommon sense, that forbids a
word of protest to drop from the signore's lips.
It is rather a certain philosophy, born of many
dull days spent on the lagoon, and many lively
hours passed with the Signora Marcelli, resulting
in some such apothegm as, " Gulls scream and
women scold, but fishing and life go on just the
same."

There is, too, the other old fisherman, whose
name I forget, who lives in the little shed of a
house next to the long wall, and who is forever
scrubbing his crab baskets, or lifting them up
and down, and otherwise disporting himself in
an idiotic and most aggravating way. He happens to own an old water-logged boat that has
the most delicious assortment of barnacles and
seaweed clinging to its sides. It is generally
piled high with great baskets, patched and
mended, with great red splotches all over them,
and bits of broken string dangling to their sides
or hanging from their open throats. There are
also a lot of rheumatic, palsied old poles that
reach over this ruin of a craft, to which are tied
still more baskets of still more delicious qualities of burnt umber and Hooker's-green moss.
Behind this boat is a sun-scorched wall of broken
brick, caressed all day by a tender old mother
of a vine, who winds her arms about it and

splashes its hot cheeks with sprays of cool shadows.

When, some years ago, I discovered this combination of boat, basket, and shadow-flecked wall, and in an unguarded moment begged the fisherman to cease work for the morning at my expense, and smoke a pipe of peace in his doorway, until I could transfer its harmonies to my canvas, I spoke hurriedly and without due consideration ; for since that time, whenever this contemporary of the original Bucentoro gets into one of my compositions, — these old fish-boats last forever and are too picturesque for even the little devils to worry over, — this same fisherman immediately dries his sponge, secures his baskets, and goes ashore, and as regularly demands backsheesh of *soldi* and fine-cut. Next summer I shall buy the boat and hire him to watch ; it will be much cheaper.

Then there are the two girls who live with their grandmother, in one end of an old tumble-down, next to the little wooden bridge that the boats lie under. She keeps a small cook shop, where she boils and then toasts, in thin strips, slices of green-skinned pumpkin, which the girls sell to the fishermen on the boats, or hawk about the *fondamenta*. As the whole pumpkin can be bought for a *lira,* you can imagine what a

96

wee bit of a copper coin it must be that pays for a fragment of its golden interior, even when the skilled labor of the old woman is added to the cost of the raw material.

Last of all are the boys, of no particular size, age, nationality, or condition ; just boys, little rascally, hatless, shoeless, shirtless, trouser — everything-less, except noise and activity. They yell like Comanches ; they crawl between the legs of your easel and look up between your knees into your face ; they steal your brushes and paints ; they cry, " Soldi, soldi, signore," until life becomes a burden ; they spend their days in one prolonged whoop of hilarity, their nights in concocting fresh deviltry, which they put into practice the moment you appear in the morning. When you throw one of them into the canal, in the vain hope that his head will stick in the mud and so he be drowned dead, half a dozen jump in after him in a delirium of enjoyment. When you turn one upside down and shake your own color tubes out of his rags, he calls upon all the saints to witness that the other fellow, the boy Beppo or Carlo, or some other " o " or " i," put them there, and that up to this very moment he was unconscious of their existence ; when you belabor the largest portion of his surface with your folding stool or

97

T-square, he is either in a state of collapse from excessive laughter or screaming with assumed agony, which lasts until he squirms himself into freedom ; then he goes wild, turning hand-springs and describing no end of geometrical figures in the air, using his stubby little nose for a centre and his grimy thumbs and outspread fingers for compasses.

All these side scenes, however, constitute only part of the family life of the Venetian fishermen. If you are up early in the morning you will see their boats moving through the narrow canals to the fish market on the Grand Canal above the Rialto, loaded to the water's edge with hundreds of bushels of crawling green crabs stowed away in the great baskets ; or piles of opalescent fish heaped upon the deck, covered with bits of sailcloth, or glistening in the morning sun. Earlier, out on the lagoon, in the gray dawn, you will see clusters of boats with the seines wide spread, the smaller dories scattered here and there, hauling or lowering the spider-skein nets.

But there is still another and a larger fishing trade, a trade not exactly Venetian, although Venice is its best market. To this belong the fishermen of Chioggia and the islands farther down the coast. These men own and man the heavier seagoing craft with the red and orange sails that make the water life of Venice unique.

Every Saturday a flock of these boats will light off the wall of the Public Garden, their beaks touching the marble rail. These are Ziem's boats — his for half a century; nobody has painted them in the afternoon light so charmingly or so truthfully. Sunday morning, after mass, they are off again, spreading their gay wings toward Chioggia. On other days one or two of these gay-plumed birds will hook a line over the cluster of spiles near the wall of the Riva, below the arsenal bridge, their sails swaying in the soft air, while their captains are buying supplies to take to the fleet twenty miles or more out at sea.

Again, sometimes in the early dawn or in the late twilight, you will see, away out in still another fishing quarter, a single figure walking slowly in the water, one arm towing his boat, the other carrying a bag. Every now and then the figure bends over, feels about with his toes, and then drops something into the bag. This is the mussel-gatherer of the lagoon. In the hot summer nights these humble toilers of the sea, with only straw mats for covering, often sleep in their boats, tethered to poles driven into the yielding mud. They can wade waist-deep over

99

many square miles of water space about Venice, although to one in a gondola, skimming over the same glassy surfaces, there seems water enough to float a ship.

These several grades of fishermen have changed but little, either in habits, costume, or the handling of their craft, since the early days of the republic. The boats, too, are almost the same in construction and equipment, as can be seen in any of the pictures of Canaletto and the painters of his time. The bows of the larger sea-craft are still broad and heavily built, the rudders big and cumbersome, with the long sweep reaching over the after-deck ; the sails are loosely hung with easily adjusted booms, to make room for the great seines which are swung to the cross-trees of the foremast. The only boat of really modern design, and this is rarely used as a fishing-boat, is the *sandolo*, a shallow skiff drawing but a few inches of water, and with both bow and stern sharp and very low, modelled originally for greater speed in racing.

Whatever changes have taken place in the political and social economy of Venice, they have affected but little these lovers of the lagoons. What mattered it to whom they paid taxes, — whether to Doge, Corsican, Austrian, or king ? There were as good fish in the sea as had ever been caught, and as long as their religion lasted, so long would people eat fish and Friday come round every week in the year.

A GONDOLA RACE

TO-DAY I am interested in watching a gondolier make his toilet in a gondola lying at my feet, for the little table holding my coffee stands on a half-round balcony that juts quite over the water-wall, almost touching the white *tenda* of the boat. From this point of vantage I look down upon his craft, tethered to a huge spile bearing the crown and monogram of the owner of the hotel. One is nobody if not noble, in Venice.

The gondolier does not see me. If he did it would not disturb him ; his boat is his home through these soft summer days and nights, and the overhanging sky gives privacy enough. A slender, graceful Venetian girl, her hair parted on one side, a shawl about her shoulders, has just brought him a bundle containing a change of clothing. She sits beside him as he dresses, and I move my chair so that I can catch the expressions of pride and delight that flit across her face while she watches the handsome, broadly built young fellow. As he stands erect in the gondola, the sunlight flashing from his wet arms, I note the fine lines of his chest, the bronzed neck and throat, and the knotted muscles along the wrist and forearm. When the white shirt with broad yellow collar and sash are adjusted and the toilet is complete, even to the straw hat worn rakishly over one ear, the girl gathers up the discarded suit, glances furtively at me, slips her hand into his for a moment, and then springs ashore, waving her handkerchief as he swings out past the Dogana, the yellow ribbons of his hat flying in the wind.

Joseph, prince among porters, catches my eye and smiles meaningly. Later, when he brings my mail, he explains that the pretty Venetian, Teresa, is the sweetheart of Pietro, the yellow and white gondolier, who serves the English lady at the Palazzo da Mula. Pietro, he tells me, rows in the regatta to-day, and these preparations are in honor of that most important event. He assures me that it will be quite the most interesting of all the regattas of the year, and that I must go early and secure a place near the stake-boat if I want to see anything of the finish. It is part of Joseph's duty and pleasure to keep you posted on everything that happens in Venice. It would distress him greatly if he thought you could obtain this information from any other source.

While we talk the Professor enters the garden from the side door of the corridor, and takes the vacant seat beside me. He, too, has come to tell me of the regatta. He is bubbling over with excitement, and insists that I shall meet him at the water-steps of the little Piazzetta near the Caffè Veneta Marina, at three o'clock, not a moment later. To-day, he says, I shall see, not the annual regatta, — that great spectacle with the Grand Canal crowded with tourists and sight-seers solidly banked from the water's edge to the very balconies, — but an oldtime contest between the two factions of the gondoliers, the Nicoletti and Castellani, a contest really of and for the Venetians themselves.

The course is to begin at the Lido, running thence to the great flour-mill up the Giudecca, and down again to the stake-boat off the Public Garden. Giuseppe is to row, and Pasquale, both famous oarsmen, and Carlo, the brother of Gaspari, who won the great regatta ; better than all, young Pietro, of the Traghetto of Santa Salute.

" Not Pietro of this *traghetto*, right here below us ?" I asked.

" Yes ; he rows with his brother Marco.

Look out for him when he comes swinging down the canal. If you have any money to wager, put it on him. Gustavo, my waiter at Florian's, says he is bound to win. His colors are yellow and white.''

This last one I knew, for had he not made his toilet, half an hour before, within sight of my table ? No wonder Teresa looked proud and happy !

While the Professor is bowing himself backward out of the garden, hat in hand, his white hair and curled mustache glistening in the sun, an oleander blossom in his buttonhole, Espero enters, also bareheaded, and begs that the Signore will use Giorgio's gondola until he can have his own boat, now at the repair-yard next to San Trovaso, scraped and pitched ; the grass on her bottom was the width of his hand. By one o'clock she would be launched again. San Trovaso, as the signore knew, was quite near the Caffè Calcina ; would he be permitted to call for him at the caffè after luncheon ? As the regatta began at three o'clock there would not be time to return again to the signore's lodging and still secure a good place at the stake-boat off the Garden.

No ; the illustrious signore would do nothing of the kind. He would take Giorgio and his gondola for the morning, and then, when the boat was finished, Espero could pick up the Professor at the Caffè Veneta Marina in the afternoon and bring him aboard Giorgio's boat on his way down the canal.

Giorgio is my stand-by when Espero is away. I often send him to my friends, those whom I love, that they may enjoy the luxury of spending a day with a man who has a score and more of sunshiny summers packed away in his heart, and not a cloud in any one of them. Tagliapietra Giorgio, of the Traghetto of Santa Salute, is his full name and address. Have Joseph call him for you some day, and your Venice will be all the more delightful because of his buoyant strength, his cheeriness, and his courtesy.

So Giorgio and I idle about the lagoon and the Giudecca, watching the flags being hoisted, the big *barche* being laden, and various other preparations for the great event of the afternoon.

After luncheon Giorgio stops at his house to change his *tenda* for the new one with the blue lining, and slips into the white suit just laundered for him. He lives a few canals away from the Calcina, with his mother, his widowed sister, and her children, in a small house with a garden all figs and oleanders. His bedroom is next to his mother's, on the second floor, over-looking the blossoms. There is a shrine above the bureau, decorated with paper flowers, and on the walls a scattering of photographs of bro-ther gondoliers, and some trophies of oars and flags. Hanging behind the door are his oilskins for wet weather, and the Tam O'Shanter cap that some former padrone has left him, as a souvenir of the good times they once had to-gether, and which Giorgio wears as a weather signal for a rainy afternoon, although the morn-ing sky may be cloudless. All gondoliers are good weather prophets.

The entire family help Giorgio with the *tenda* — the old mother carrying the side curtains, warm from her flatiron, and chubby Beppo, bareheaded and barefooted, bringing up the rear with the little blue streamer that on gala days floats from the gondola's lamp-socket forward, which on other days is always filled with flow-ers.

Then we are off, picking our way down the narrow canal, waiting here and there for the big *barche* to pass, laden with wine or fruit, un-til we shoot out into the broad waters of the Giudecca.

You see at a glance that Venice is astir. All along the Zattere, on every wood-boat, *barco,*

and barge, on every bridge, balcony, and house-
top, abreast the wide *fondamenta* fronting the
great warehouses, and away down the edge
below the Redentore, the people are swarming
like flies. Out on the Giudecca, anchored to
the channel spiles, is a double line of boats of
every conceivable description, from a toy *sandolo* to a steamer's barge. These lie stretched
out on the water like two great sea-serpents,
their heads facing the garden, their tails curving toward the Redentore.

Between these two sea-monsters, with their
flashing scales of a thousand umbrellas, is an
open roadway of glistening silver.

Giorgio swings across to the salt-warehouses
above the Dogana and on down and over to the
Riva. Then there is a shout ahead, a red and
white *tenda* veers a point, comes close, backs
water, and the Professor springs in.

"Here, Professor, here beside me on the
cushions!" I call out. "Draw back the curtains, Giorgio. And, Espero, hurry ahead and
secure a place near the stake-boat. We will be
there in ten minutes."

The Professor was a sight to cheer the heart
of an amateur yachtsman out for a holiday.
He had changed his suit of the morning for a
small straw hat trimmed with red, an enor-

mous field-glass with a strap over his shoulder, and a short velvet coat that had once done service as a smoking-jacket. His mustachios were waxed into needle points. The occasion had for him all the novelty of the first spring meeting at Longchamps, or a race off Cowes, and he threw himself into its spirit with the gusto of a boy.

"What colors are you flying, *mon capitaine?* Blue? Never!" noticing Giorgio's streamer. "Pasquale's color is blue, and he will be half a mile astern when Pietro is round the stake-boat. Vive le jaune! Vive Pietro!" and out came a yellow rag — Pietro's color — bearing a strong resemblance to the fragment of some old silk curtain. It settled at a glance all doubt as to the Professor's sympathies in the coming contest.

The day was made for a regatta, — a cool, crisp, bracing October day; a day of white clouds and turquoise skies, of flurries of soft winds that came romping down the lagoon, turned for a moment in play, and then went scampering out to sea; a day of dazzling sun, of brilliant distances, of clear-cut outlines, black shadows, and flashing lights.

As we neared the Public Garden the crowd grew denser; the cries of the gondoliers were incessant; even Giorgio's skilful oar was taxed to the utmost to avoid the polluting touch of an underbred *sandolo,* or the still greater calamity of a collision — really an unpardonable sin with a gondolier. Every now and then a chorus of yells, charging every crime in the decalogue, would be hurled at some landsman whose oar "crabbed," or at some nondescript craft filled with "barbers and cooks," to quote Giorgio, who in forcing a passage had become hopelessly entangled.

The only clear water space was the ribbon of silver beginning away up near the Redentore, between the tails of the two sea monsters, and ending at the stake-boat. Elsewhere, on both sides, from the Riva to San Giorgio, and as far as the wall of the Garden, was a dense floating mass of human beings, cheering, singing, and laughing, waving colors, and calling out the names of their favorites in rapid *crescendo.*

The spectacle on land was also unique. The balustrade of the broad walk of the Public Garden was a huge flower-bed of blossoming hats and fans, spotted with myriads of parasols in full bloom. Bunches of over-ripe boys hung in the trees, or dropped one by one into the arms of gendarmes below. The palaces along the Riva were a broad ribbon of color with a binding of black coats and hats. The wall of

San Giorgio fronting the barracks was fringed with the yellow legs and edged with the white fatigue caps of two regiments. Even over the roofs and tower of the church itself specks of sight-seers were spattered here and there, as if the joyous wind in some mad frolic had caught them up in very glee, and as suddenly showered them on cornice, sill, and dome.

Beyond all this, away out on the lagoon, toward the islands, the red-sailed fishing-boats hurried in for the finish, their canvas aflame against the deepening blue. Over all the sunlight danced and blazed and shimmered, gilding and bronzing the roof-jewels of San Marco, flashing from oar blade, brass, and *ferro*, silvering the pigeons whirling deliriously in the intoxicating air, making glad and gay and happy every soul who breathed the breath of this joyous Venetian day.

None of all this was lost upon the Professor. He stood in the bow drinking in the scene, sweeping his spy-glass round like a weathervane, straining his eyes up the Giudecca to catch the first glimpse of the coming boats, picking out faces under flaunting parasols, and waving aloft his yellow rag when some gondola swept by flying Pietro's colors, or some boatload of friends saluted in passing.

Suddenly there came down on the shifting wind, from far up the Giudecca, a sound like the distant baying of a pack of hounds, and as suddenly died away. Then the roar of a thousand throats, caught up by a thousand more about us, broke on the air, as a boatman, perched on a masthead, waved his hat.

"Here they come! Viva Pietro! Viva Pasquale! — Castellani! — Nicoletti! — Pietro!"

The dense mass rose and fell in undulations, like a great carpet being shaken, its colors tossing in the sunlight. Between the thicket of *ferri*, away down the silver ribbon, my eye caught two little specks of yellow capping two white figures. Behind these, almost in line, were two similar dots of blue; farther away other dots, hardly distinguishable, on the horizon line.

The gale became a tempest — the roar was deafening; women waved their shawls in the air; men, swinging their hats, shouted themselves hoarse. The yellow specks developed into handkerchiefs bound to the heads of Pietro and his brother Marco; the blues were those of Pasquale and his mate.

Then, as we strain our eyes, the two tails of the sea monster twist and clash together, closing in upon the string of rowers as they disappear in the dip behind San Giorgio, only to reappear in full sight, Pietro half a length ahead, straining every sinew, his superb arms swinging like a flail, his lithe body swaying in splendid, springing curves, the water rushing from his oar blade, his brother bending aft in perfect rhythm.

" Pietro ! *Pietro !* " came the cry, shrill and clear, drowning all other sounds, and a great field of yellow burst into flower all over the lagoon, from San Giorgio to the Garden. The people went wild. If before there had been only a tempest, now there was a cyclone. The waves of blue and yellow surged alternately above the heads of the throng as Pasquale or Pietro gained or lost a foot. The Professor grew red and pale by turns, his voice broken to a whisper with continued cheering, the yellow rag streaming above his head, all the blood of his ancestors blazing in his face.

The contesting boats surged closer. You could now see the rise and fall of Pietro's superb chest, the steel-like grip of his hands, and could outline the curves of his thighs and back. The ends of the yellow handkerchief, bound close about his head, were flying in the wind. His stroke was long and sweeping, his full weight on the oar. Pasquale's stroke was short and quick, like the thrust of a spur.

Now they are abreast; Pietro's eyes are blazing, Pasquale's teeth are set. Both crews are doing their utmost. The yells are demoniac. Even the women are beside themselves with excitement.

Suddenly, when within five hundred yards of the goal, Pasquale turns his head to his mate; there is an answering cry, and then, as if some unseen power had lent its strength, Pasquale's boat shoots half a length ahead, slackens, falls back, gains again, now an inch, now a foot, now clear of Pietro's bow, and on, on, lashing the water, surging forward, springing with every gain, cheered by a thousand throats, past the red tower of San Giorgio, past the channel of spiles off the Garden, past the red buoy near the great warship, — one quick, sustained, blistering stroke, — until the judge's flag drops from his hand, and the great race is won.

"A true knight, a gentleman every inch of him!" called out the Professor, forgetting that he had staked all his *soldi* on Pietro. "Fairly won, Pasquale."

In the whirl of the victory, I had forgotten Pietro, my gondolier of the morning. The poor fellow was sitting in the bow of his boat, his head in his hands, wiping his forehead and throat, the tears streaming down his cheeks.

His brother sat beside him. In the gladness and disappointment of the hour, no one of the crowd around him seemed to think of the hero of five minutes before. Not so Giorgio, who was beside himself with grief over Pietro's defeat, and who had not taken his eyes from his face. In an instant more he sprang forward, calling out, "No! no! Brava Pietro!" Espero joining in as if with a common impulse, and both forcing their gondolas close to Pietro's.

A moment more and Giorgio was over the rail of Pietro's boat, patting his back, stroking his head, comforting him as you would think only a woman could — but then you do not know Giorgio. Pietro lifted up his face and looked into Giorgio's eyes with an expression so woe-begone, and full of such intense suffering, that Giorgio instinctively flung his arm around the great splendid fellow's neck. Then came a few broken words, a tender caressing stroke of Giorgio's hand, a drawing of Pietro's head down on his breast as if it had been a girl's, and then, still comforting him — telling him over and over again how superbly he had rowed, how the next time he would win, how he had made a grand second —

Giorgio bent his head — *and kissed him.*

When Pietro, a moment later, pulled himself

together and stood erect in his boat, with eyes still wet, the look on his face was as firm and determined as ever.

Nobody laughed. It did not shock the crowd; nobody thought Giorgio unmanly or foolish, or Pietro silly or effeminate. The infernal Anglo-Saxon custom of always wearing a mask of reserve, if your heart breaks, has never reached these people.

As for the Professor, who looked on quietly, I think — yes, I am quite sure — that a little jewel of a tear squeezed itself up through his punctilious, precise, ever exact and courteous body, and glistened long enough on his eyelids to wet their lashes. Then the bright sun and the joyous wind caught it away. Dear old relic of a bygone time! How gentle a heart beats under your well-brushed, threadbare coat!

SOME VENETIAN CAFFÈS

EVERY one in Venice has his own particular caffè, according to his own particular needs, sympathies, or tastes. All the artists, architects, and musicians meet at Florian's ; all the Venetians go to the Quadri ; the Germans and late Austrians, to the Bauer-Grünwald ; the stay-over-nights, to the Oriental on the Riva ; the stevedores, to the Veneta Marina below the Arsenal ; and my dear friend Luigi and his fellow tramps, to a little hole in the wall on the Via Garibaldi.

These caffès are scattered everywhere, from the Public Garden to the Mestre bridge ; all kinds of caffès for all kinds of people, — rich, not so rich, poor, poorer, and the very poorest. Many of them serve only a cup of coffee, two little flat lumps of sugar, a hard, brown roll, and a glass of water — always a glass of water. Some add a few syrups and cordials, with a siphon of seltzer. Others indulge in the cheaper wines of the country, Brindisi, Chianti, and the like, and are then known as wine shops. Very few serve any spirits, except a spoonful of cognac with the coffee. Water is the universal beverage, and in summer this is cooled by ice and enriched by simple syrups of peach, orange, and raspberry. Spirits are rarely taken, and intemperance is practically unknown. In an experience of many years, I have not seen ten drunken men, — never one drunken woman, — and only in September, when the strong wine from Brindisi is brought in bulk and sold over the boat's rail, literally by the bucket, to whoever will buy.

In the *ristoranti* — caffès, in our sense — is served an array of eatables that would puzzle the most expert of gourmands. There will be macaroni, of course, in all forms, and *risotto* in a dozen different ways, and soups with weird, uncanny little devil-fish floating about in them, and salads of every conceivable green thing that can be chopped up in a bowl and drowned in olive oil; besides an assortment of cheeses with individualities of perfume that beggar any similar collection outside of Holland.

Some of these caffès are so much a part of Venice and Venetian life, that you are led to believe that they were founded by the early Doges and are coeval with the Campanile or the Library. Somebody, of course, must know when they first began setting out tables on the Piazza in front of Florian's, or at the Quadri opposite, or yet again at the Caffè al Cavallo, near San Giovanni e Paulo, and at scores of others ; but I confess I do not. If you ask the head waiter, who really ought to know (for he must have been born in one of the upper rooms, — he certainly never leaves the lower ones), he shrugs his shoulders in a hopeless way and sheds the inquiry with a despairing gesture, quite as if you had asked who laid out San Marco, or who drove the piles under Saint Theodore.

There is, I am convinced, no real, permanent, steady proprietor in any of these caffès — none that one ever sees. There must be, of course, somebody who assumes ownership, and who for a time really believes that he has a proprietary interest in the chairs and tables about him. After a while, however, he gets old and dies, and is buried over in Campo Santo, and even his name is forgotten. When this happens, and it is eminently proper that it should, another ·tenant takes possession, quite as the pigeons do of an empty carving over the door of the king's palace.

But the caffè keeps on : the same old marble-top tables ; the same old glass-covered pictures, with the impossible Turkish houris listening to

the improbable gentleman in baggy trousers ;
the same serving-counter, with the row of cordials in glass bottles with silver stoppers. The
same waiters, too, hurry about — they live on
for centuries — wearing the same coats and
neckties, and carrying the same napkins. I myself have never seen a dead waiter, and, now I
happen to think of it, I have never heard of one.

The head waiter is, of course, supreme. He
it is who adds up on his fingers the sum of your
extravagances, who takes your money and
dives down into his own pocket for the change.
He and his assistants are constantly running in
and out, vanishing down subterranean stairs, or
disappearing through swinging doors, with the
agility of Harlequin ; you never know where or
why, until they pop out again, whirling trays
held high over their heads, or bearing in both
hands huge waiters loaded with dishes.

The *habitués* of these caffès are as interesting
as the caffès themselves. The Professor comes,
of course ; you always know where to find *him*.
And the youthful contessa ! She of the uncertain age, with hair bleached to a light law calf,
and a rose-colored veil ! And here comes, too,
every distinguished or notorious person of high
or low degree at the moment in Venice ; you
have only to take a chair at Florian's and be

patient, — they are sure to appear before the music is over. There is the sister of the arch-duke, with the straight-backed, pipe-stem-legged officer acting as gentleman in waiting; and he does *wait*, standing bolt upright like a sergeant on dress parade, sometimes an hour, for her to sit down. There is the Spanish grandee, with a palace for the season (an upper floor with an entrance on a side canal), whose gondoliers wear flaming scarlet, with a crest embossed on brass dinner-plates for arm ornaments; one of these liveried attendants always dogs the grandee to the caffè, so as to be ready to pull his chair out when his excellency sits down. Then there are the Royal Academician, in gray tweed knickerbockers, travelling *incognito* with two friends; the fragments of an American linen-duster brigade, with red guide-books and faces, in charge of a special agent; besides scores of others of every nationality and rank. They are all at Florian's some time during the day.

You will see there, too, if you are familiar with the inside workings of a favorite caffè, an underground life of intrigue or mystery, in which Gustavo or Florio has a hand — often upon a *billet-doux* concealed within the folds of a napkin; not to mention the harmless distribution, once in a while, of smuggled cigarettes fresh from Cairo.

Poor Gustavo! The government brought him to book not long ago. For many years he had supplied his patrons, and with delicious Egyptians, too! One night Gustavo disappeared, escorted by two gendarmes from the Department of Justice. Next morning the judge said, "Whereas, according to the accounts kept by the Department of Customs, the duties and expenses due the king on the cigarettes unlawfully sold by the prisoner for years past aggregate two thousand three hundred and ten *lire;* and whereas, the savings of the prisoner for ten years past, and at the moment deposited to his individual credit in the Banco Napoli, amount to exactly two thousand three hundred and ten *lire;* therefore, it is ordered, that a sight draft for the exact amount be drawn in favor of the king." This would entitle Gustavo to the pure air of the Piazza; otherwise? — well, otherwise not. Within a week Gustavo was again whirling his tray, a little grayer, perhaps, and a little wiser, — certainly poorer. Thus does a tyrannical government oppress its people!

These caffès of the piazza, with their iced carafes, white napkins, and little silver coffeepots, are the caffès of the rich.

SOME VENETIAN CAFFES

The caffè of the poor is sometimes afloat. No matter how early you are out in the morning, this floating caffè — the cook-boat — has its fire lighted, and the savory smell of its cuisine drifts over the lagoon, long before your gondola rounds the Dogana. When you come alongside you find a charcoal brazier heating a pan of savory fish and a large pot of coffee, and near by a basketful of rolls, fresh and warm, from a still earlier baker. There are peaches, too, and a hamper of figs. The cook-boat is tended by two men; one cooks and serves, and the other rows, standing in the stern, looking anxiously for customers, and calling out in stentorian tones that all the delicacies of the season are now being fried, broiled, and toasted, and that for the infinitesimal sum of ten *soldi* you can breakfast like a doge.

If you are just out of the lagoon, your blood tingling with the touch of the sea, your face aglow with your early morning bath, answer the cry of one of these floating kitchens, and eat a breakfast with the rising sun lighting your forehead and the cool breath of the lagoon across your cheek. It may be the salt air and the early plunge that make the coffee so savory, the fish and rolls so delicious, and the fruit so refreshing; or it may be because the fish were

123

wriggling in the bottom of the boat half an hour earlier, the coffee only at the first boiling, and the fruit, bought from a passing boat, still damp with the night's dew !

The caffè of the poorest is wherever there is a crowd. It generally stands on three iron legs under one of the trees down the Via Garibaldi, or over by the landing of the Dogana, or beneath the shade of some awning, or up a back court. The old fellow who bends over the hot earthen dish, supported on these legs, slowly stirring a mess of kidneys or an indescribable stew, is cook, head waiter, and proprietor all in one. Every now and then he fishes out some delicate tidbit, — a miniature octopus, perhaps (called *fulpe*), a little sea-horror, all legs and claws, which he sprawls out on a bit of brown paper and lays on the palm of your left hand, assuming, clearly, that you have all the knives and forks that you need, on your right.

Once in a while a good Bohemian discovers some out-of-the-way place up a canal or through a twisted *calle* that delights him with its cuisine, its cellar, or its cosiness, and forever after he preëmpts it as *his* caffè. I know half a dozen such discoveries, — one somewhere near San Giorgio degli Schiavoni, where the men play bowls in a long, narrow alley, under wide-spreading trees, cramped up between high buildings; and another, off the Merceria, where the officers smoke and lounge; and still another, quite my own, the Càffè Calcina. This last is on the Rio San Vio, and looks out on the Giudecca, just below San Rosario. You would never suspect it of being a caffè at all, until you had dodged under the little roof of the porch to escape the heat, and opening the side door found yourself in a small, plainly furnished room with little marble-top tables, each decorated with a Siamese-twin salt-cellar holding a pinch of salt and of pepper. Even then it is a very common sort of caffè, and not at all the place you would care to breakfast in twice; that is, not until you had followed the demure waiter through a narrow passage and out into a square *patio* splashed with yellow-green light and cooled by overlacing vines. Then you realize that this same square patch of ground is one of the few restful spots of the wide earth.

It is all open to the sky except for a great arbor of grape leaves covering the whole area, beneath which, on the cool, moist ground, stand half a dozen little tables covered with snow-white cloths. At one side is a shelter, from behind which come certain mysterious noises of fries and broils. All about are big, green-painted

boxes of japonicas, while at one end the oleanders thrust their top branches through the overhanging leaves of the arbor, waving their blossoms defiantly in the blazing sun. Beneath this
grateful shelter you sit and loaf and invite your
soul, and your best friend, too, if he happens to
be that sort of man.

.After having congratulated yourself on your
discovery and having become a daily *habitué*
of the delightful *patio*, you find that you have
really discovered the Grand Canal or the Rialto
bridge. To your great surprise, the Caffè Calcina has been the favorite resort of good Bohemians for nearly a century. You learn that
Turner painted his sunset sketches from its upper windows, and that dozens of more modern
English painters have lived in the rooms above;
that Whistler and Rico and scores of others
have broken bread and had toothsome omelets
under its vines; and, more precious than all,
that Ruskin and Browning have shared many
a bottle of honest Chianti with these same oleanders above their heads, and this, too, in the
years when the Sage of Brantwood was teach-
ing the world to love his Venice, and the great
poet was singing songs that will last as long as
the language.

ON THE HOTEL STEPS

IF you drink your early coffee as I do, in
the garden under the oleanders, overlooking
the water-landing of the hotel, and linger long
enough over your fruit, you will conclude before many days that a large part of the life of
Venice can be seen from the hotel steps. You
may behold the great row of gondolas at the
traghetto near by, ranged side by side, awaiting
their turn, and here and there, tied to the spiles
outside the line, the more fortunate boats whose
owners serve some sight-seer by the week, or
some native padrone by the month, and are
thus free of the daily routine of the *traghetto*,
and free, too, from our old friend Joseph's summoning voice.

You will be delighted at the good humor and
good fellowship which animate this group of
gondoliers, their ringing songs and hearty laughter, their constant care of the boats, their daily
sponging and polishing ; and now and then, I
regret to say, your ears will be assailed by a
quarrel, so fierce, so loud, and so full of vindic-

127

tive energy, that you will start from your seat
in instant expectation of the gleam of a stiletto,
until by long experience you learn how harmless are both the bark and bite of a gondolier,
and how necessary as a safety valve, to accused
and accuser as well, is the unlimited air space
of the Grand Canal.

You will also come into closer contact with
Joseph, prince among porters, and patron saint
of this Traghetto of Santa Salute. There is another saint, of course, shaded by its trellised
vines, framed in tawdry gilt, protected from the
weather by a wooden hood, and lighted at night
by a dim lamp hanging before it; but, for all
that, Joseph is supreme as protector, refuge, and
friend.

Joseph, indeed, is more than this. He is
the patron saint and father confessor of every
wayfarer, of whatever tongue. Should a copper-
colored gentleman mount the steps of the hotel
landing, attired in calico trousers, a short jacket
of pea-green silk, and six yards of bath towel-
ling about his head, Joseph instantly addresses
him in broken Hindoostanee, sending his rattan
chairs and paper boxes to a room overlooking
the shady court, and placing a boy on the rug
outside, ready to spring when the copper-col-
ored gentleman claps his hands. Does another

distinguished foreigner step from the gondola, attended by two valets with a block-tinned trunk, half a score of hat-boxes, bags, and bundles, four umbrellas, and a dozen sticks, Joseph at once accosts him in most excellent English, and has ordered a green-painted tub rolled into his room before he has had time to reach the door of his apartment. If another equally distinguished traveller alights on the marble slab, wearing a Bond Street ulster, a slouch hat, and a ready-made summer suit, with yellow shoes, and carrying an Alpine staff (so useful in Venice) branded with illegible letters chasing each other spirally up and down the wooden handle, Joseph takes his measure at a glance. He knows it is his first trip *en Cook*, and that he will want the earth, and instantly decides that so far as concerns himself he shall have it, including a small, round, convenient little portable which he immediately places behind the door to save the marble hearth. So with the titled Frenchman, wife, maid, and canary bird; the haughty Austrian, his sword in a buckskin bag; the stolid German with the stout helpmate and one satchel, or the Spaniard with two friends and no baggage at all.

Joseph knows them all, — their conditions, wants, economies, meannesses, escapades, and subterfuges. Does he not remember how you haggled over the price of your room, and the row you made when your shoes were mixed up with the old gentleman's on the floor above? Does he not open the door in the small hours, when you slink in, the bell sounding like a toc- sin at your touch? Is he not rubbing his eyes and carrying the candle that lights you down to the corridor door, the only exit from the hotel after midnight, when you had hoped to escape by the garden, and dared not look up at the balcony above?

Here also you will often meet the Professor. Indeed, he is breakfasting with me in this same garden this very morning. It is the first time I have seen him since the memorable day of the regatta, when Pasquale won the prize and the old fellow lost his *soldi*.

He has laid aside his outing costume — the short jacket, beribboned hat, and huge field- glass — and is gracing my table clothed in what he is pleased to call his "garb of tuition," worn to-day because of a pupil who expects him at nine o'clock, — "a horrid old German woman from Prague," he calls her. This garb is the same old frock coat of many summers, the well- ironed silk hat, and the limp glove dangling from his hand or laid like a crumpled leaf on the cloth beside him. The coat, held snug to the waist by a single button, always bulges out over the chest, the two frogs serving as pockets. From these depths, near the waist line, the Professor now and then drags up a great silk handkerchief, either red or black, as the week's wash may permit, for I have never known of his owning more than two!

To-day, below the bulge of this too large handkerchief swells yet another enlargement, to which my guest, tapping it significantly with his finger-tips, refers in a most mysterious way as "a very great secret," but without unbosoming to me either its cause or its mystery. When the cigarettes are lighted he drops his hand deep into his one-buttoned coat, unloads the handkerchief, and takes out a little volume bound in vellum, a book he has promised me for weeks. This solves the mystery and effaces the bulge.

One of the delights of knowing the Professor well is to see him handle a book that he loves. He has a peculiar way of smoothing the sides before opening it, as one would a child's hand, and of always turning the leaves as though he were afraid of hurting the back, caressing them one by one with his fingers, quite as a bird plumes its feathers. And he is always bringing a new book to light; one of his charming

idiosyncrasies is the hunting about in odd corners for just such odd volumes.

"Out of print now, my dear fellow. You
can't buy it for money. This is the only copy
in Venice that I could borrow for love. See the
chapters on these very fellows — these gondoliers," pointing to the *traghetto*. "Sometimes,
when I hear their quarrels, I wonder if they ever
remember that their guild is as old as the days
of the Doges, a fossil survival, unique, perhaps,
in the history of this or of any other country."

While the Professor nibbles at the crescents
and sips his coffee, pausing now and then to
read me passages taken at random from the little volume in his hands, I watch the procession
of gondolas from the *traghetto*, like a row of
cabs taking their turn, as Joseph's "*a una*"
or "*due*" rings out over the water. One after
another they steal noiselessly up and touch the
water-steps, Joseph helping each party into its
boat : the German baroness with the two poo-
dles and a silk parasol ; the poor fellow from the
Engadine, with the rugs and an extra overcoat,
his mother's arm about him — not many more
sunshiny days for him ; the bevy of joyous
young girls in summer dresses and sailor hats,
and the two college boys in white flannels, the
chaperon in the *next* boat. "Ah, these sweet

young Americans, these naïve countrywomen of yours!" whispers the Professor; "how exquisitely bold!" Last, the painter, with his trap and a big canvas, which he lifts in as carefully as if it had a broken rib, and then turns quickly face in; "An old Doge," you say to yourself, "unfinished, of course!"

Presently a tall, finely formed gondolier in dark blue, with a red sash, whirls the *ferro* of his boat close to the landing-steps, and a graceful, dignified woman, past middle life, but still showing traces of great beauty, steps in, and sinks upon the soft cushions.

The Professor rises like a grand duke receiving a princess, brings one arm to a salute, places the other over his heart, and makes a bow that carries the conviction of profound respect and loyalty in its every curve. The lady acknowledges it with a gracious bend of her head, and a smile which shows her appreciation of its sincerity.

"An English lady of rank who spends her Octobers here," says the Professor, when he regains his seat. He had remained standing until the gondola had disappeared — such old-time observances are part of his religion.

"Did you notice her gondolier? That is Giovanni, the famous oarsman. Let me tell you

133

the most delicious story ! Oh, the childish sim-
plicity of these men ! You would say, would
you not, that he was about forty years of age ?
You saw, too, how broad and big he was ?
Well, *mon ami*, not only is he the strongest
oarsman in Venice, but he has proved it, for he
has won the annual regatta, the great one on
the Grand Canal, for five consecutive summers !
This, you know, gives him the title of ' Em-
peror.' Now, there is a most charming signora
whom he has served for years, — she always
spends her summers here, — whom, I assure
you, Giovanni idolizes, and over whom he
watches exactly as if she were both his child
and his queen. Well, one day last year," here
the Professor's face cracked into lines of sup-
pressed mirth, " Giovanni asked for a day's
leave, and went over to Mestre to bid good-by
to some friends *en route* for Milan. The Brindisi wine — the *vino forte ;* oh, that devilish
wine ! you know it ! — had just reached Mestre. It only comes in September, and lasts but
a few weeks. Of course Giovanni must have
his grand outing, and three days later Signor
Giovanni-the-Strong presented himself again at
the door of the apartment of his signora, sober,
but limp as a rag. The signora, grand dame
as she was, refused to see him, sending word

by her maid that she would not hear a word from him until the next day. Now, what do you think this great strong fellow did? He went home, threw himself on the bed, turned his face to the wall, and for half the night cried like a baby! Think of it! like a baby! His wife could not get him to eat a mouthful.

"The next day, of course, the signora forgave him. There was nothing else to be done, for, as she said to me afterwards, 'What? Venice without Giovanni! Mon Dieu!'"

The Professor throws away the end of his last cigarette and begins gathering up his hat and the one unmated, lonely glove. No living soul ever yet saw him put this on. Sometimes he thrusts in his two fingers, as if fully intending to bury his entire hand, and then you see an expression of doubt and hesitancy cross his face, denoting a change of mind, as he crumples it carelessly, or pushes it into his coattail pocket to keep company with its fictitious mate.

At this moment Espero raises his head out of his gondola immediately beneath us. Everything is ready, he says: the sketch trap, extra canvas, fresh siphon of seltzer, ice, *fiasca* of Chianti, Gorgonzola, all but the rolls, which he will get at the baker's on our way over to the

Giudecca, where I am to work on the sketch begun yesterday.

" Ah, that horrid old German woman from Prague ! " sighs the Professor. " If I could only go with you ! "

OPEN–AIR MARKETS

SOMETIMES, in early autumn, on the lagoon behind the Rendentore, you may overtake a curious craft, half barge, half gondola, rowed by a stooping figure in cowl and frock.

Against the glow of the fading twilight this quaint figure — standing in the stern of his flower-laden boat, swaying to the rhythm of his oar — will recall so vividly the time when that other

" Dumb old servitor . . . went upward with the flood,"

that you cannot help straining your eyes in a vain search for the fair face of the lily maid of Astolat hidden among the blossoms. Upon looking closer you discover that it is only the gardener of the convent grounds, on his way to the market above the Rialto.

If you continue your course, crossing the Giudecca, or if you happen to be coming from Murano or the Lido, you will pass dozens of other boats, loaded to the water's edge with baskets upon baskets of peaches, melons, and figs, or great heaps of green vegetables, dashed here and there with piles of blood-red tomatoes. All these boats are pointing their bows towards the Ponte Paglia, the bridge on the Riva between the Doges' Palace and the prison, the one next the Bridge of Sighs. Here, in the afternoons preceding market days, they unship their masts or rearrange their cargoes, taking off the top baskets if too high to clear the arch. Ponte Paglia is the best point of entrance from the Grand Canal, because it is the beginning of that short cut, through a series of smaller canals, to the fruit market above the Rialto bridge. The market opens at daybreak.

Many of these boats come from Malamocco, on the south, a small island this side of Chioggia, and from beyond the island known as the Madonna of the Seaweed, named after a curious figure sheltered by a copper umbrella. Many of them come from Torcello, that most ancient of the Venetian settlements, and from the fruit-raising country back of it, for all Torcello is one great orchard, with every landing-wharf piled full of its products. Here you can taste a fig so delicately ripe that it fairly melts in your mouth, and so sensitive that it withers and turns black almost with the handling. Here

138

are rose-pink peaches the size of small melons, and golden lemons the size of peaches. Here are pomegranates that burst open from very lusciousness, and white grapes that hang in masses, and melons and plums in heaps, and all sorts of queer little round things that you never taste but once, and never want to taste again.

These fruit gardens and orchards in the suburbs of Venice express the very waste and wantonness of the climate. There is no order in setting out the fruit, no plan in growing, no system in gathering. The trees thrive wherever they happen to have taken root — here a peach, here a pear, there a pomegranate. The vines climb the trunks and limbs, or swing off to tottering poles and crumbling walls. The watermelons lie flat on their backs in the blazing sun, flaunting their big leaves in your face, their tangled creepers in everybody's way and under everybody's feet. The peaches cling in matted clusters, and the figs and plums weigh down the drooping branches.

If you happen to have a *lira* about you, and own besides a bushel basket, you can exchange the coin for that measure of peaches. Two *lire* will load your gondola half full of melons ; three *lire* will pack it with grapes ; four *lire* — well, you must get a larger boat.

139

OPEN–AIR MARKETS

When the boats are loaded at the orchards and poled through the grass-lined canals, reaching the open water of the lagoon, escaping the swarms of naked boys begging backsheesh of fruit from their cargoes, you will notice that each craft stops at a square box, covered by an awning and decorated with a flag, anchored out in the channel, or moored to a cluster of spiles. This is the Dogana of the lagoon, and every basket, crate, and box must be inspected and counted by the official in the flat cap with the tarnished gilt band, who commands this box of a boat, for each individual peach, plum, and pear must help pay its share of the public debt.

This floating custom-house is one of many beads, strung at intervals a mile apart, completely encircling Venice. It is safe to say that nothing that crows, bleats, or clucks, nothing that feeds, clothes, or is eaten, ever breaks through this charmed circle without leaving some portion of its value behind. This creditor takes its pound of flesh the moment it is due, and has never been known to wait.

Where the deep-water channels are shifting, and there is a possibility of some more knowing and perhaps less honest market craft slipping past in the night, a government deputy silently steals over the shallow lagoon in a rowboat,

sleeping in his blanket, his hand on his mus-
ket, and rousing at the faintest sound of row-
lock or sail. Almost hourly one of these night
hawks overhauls other strollers of the lagoon
in the by-passages outside the city limits, —
some smuggler, with cargo carefully covered,
or perhaps a pair of lovers in a gondola with too
closely drawn *tenda*. There is no warning sound
to the unwary ; only the gurgle of a slowly
moving oar, then the muzzle of a breech-loader
thrust into one's eyes, behind which frowns
an ugly, determined face, peering from out the
folds of a heavy boat-cloak. It is the deputy's
way of asking for smuggled cigarettes, but it is
so convincing a way as to admit of no discussion. Ever afterward the unfortunate victim, if
he be of honest intent, can not only detect a
police-boat from a fishing-yawl, but remembers
also to keep a light burning in his lamp-socket
forward, as evidence of his honesty.

When the cargoes of the market-boats are
inspected, the duties paid, and the passage made
under Ponte Paglia, or through the many name-
less canals if the approach is made from the
Campo Santo side of the city, the boats swarm
up to the fruit market above the Rialto, rounding up one after another, and discharging their
contents like trucks at a station, the men piling

the baskets in great mounds on the broad stone quay.

After the inhabitants have pounced upon these heaps and mounds and pyramids of baskets and crates, and have carried them away, the market is swept and scoured as clean as a china plate, not even a peach-pit being left to tell the tale of the morning. Then this greater market shrinks into the smaller one, the little fruit market of the Rialto, which is never closed, day or night.

This little market — or rather, the broad street forming its area, broad for this part of Venice — is always piled high with the products of orchard, vineyard, and garden, shaded all day by huge awnings, so closely stretched that only the sharpest and most lance-like of sunbeams can cut their way into the coolness below. At night the market is lighted by flaring torches illumining the whole surrounding *campo*.

As for the other, smaller stands and shops about the city, they are no less permanent fixtures, and keep equally bad hours. No matter how late you stroll down the Zattere or elbow your way along the Merceria, when every other place is closed, you will come upon a blazing lamp lighting up a heap of luscious fruit, in its season the comfort and sustenance of Venice.

Then there are the other markets, — the wood market of the Giudecca, the fish market below the Rialto bridge, and the shops and stalls scattered throughout the city.

The wood market, a double row of boats moored in midstream and stretching up the broad waterway, is behind the Salute and the salt warehouses: great, heavy, Dutch-bowed boats, with anchor chains hanging from the open mouths of dolphins carved on the planking; long, sharp bowsprits, painted red, and great overhanging green rudder-sweeps swaying a rudder half as large as a barn door. Aft there is always an awning stretched to the mainmast, under which lies the captain, generally sound asleep.

When you board one of these floating woodyards, and, rousing the Signor Capitano, beg permission to spread your sketch-awning on the forward deck out of everybody's way, you will not only get the best point of view from which to paint the exquisite domes and towers of the beautiful Santa Maria della Salute, but, if you sit all day at work, with the deck wet and cool beneath your feet, and listen to the barter and sale going on around, you will become familiar

143

with the workings of the market itself. You
will find all these boats loaded under and above
deck with sticks of wood cut about the size
of an axe handle, tied in bundles that can be
tucked under one's arm. These are sold over
the ship's side to the pedlers, who boat them
off to their shops ashore. All day long these
hucksters come and go, some for a boat load,
some for a hundred bundles, some for only one.
When the purchase is important, and the count
reaches, say, an even hundred, there is always
a squabble over the tally. The captain, of
course, counts, and so does the mate, and so
does the buyer. As soon as the controversy
reaches the point where there is nothing left
but to brain the captain with one of his own
fagots, he gives in, and throws an extra bundle
into the boat, however honest may have been
the count before. The instantaneous good humor developed all around at the concession is
possible only among a people who quarrel as
easily as they sing.

Wood is really almost the only fuel in Venice. Coal is too costly, and the means of utiliz-
ing it too complicated. What is wanted is a
handful of embers over which to boil a pot of
coffee or warm a soup, a little fire at a time, and
as little as possible, for, unlike many another

commodity, fuel is a bugbear of economy to the Venetian. He rarely worries over his rent; it is his wood bill that keeps him awake nights.

Above the fruit market near the Rialto is the new fish market, a modern horror of cast iron and ribbed glass. (Oh, if the polluting touch of so-called modern progress could only be kept away from this rarest of cities!) Here are piled and hung and spread out the endless varieties of fish and sea foods from the lagoons and the deep waters beyond; great halibut, with bellies of Japanese porcelain, millions of minnows, like heaps of wet opals with shavings of pearl, crabs, *fulpe*, mussels, and the spoils of the marshes. Outside, along the canal, are ranged the market-boats, with their noses flattened against the stone quay, their sails clewed up, freeing the decks, the crews bending under huge baskets.

Fish is the natural flesh food of the Venetian, fresh every morning, and at a price for even the poorest. If there is not money enough for a clean slice cut through the girth of a sea monster, for a broil, less than a *soldo* will buy a handful of little nondescripts like fat spiders, for soup, or a pint of pebble-like mussels with which to savor a stew.

145

ON RAINY DAYS

THE wind blows east! All night long the thunder of the surf breaking along the Lido has reverberated through the deserted streets and abandoned canals of Venice.

From your window you see the fair goddess of the Dogana, tired out with the whirling winds, clinging in despair to the golden ball, — her sail flying westward, her eyes strained in search of the lost sun. You see, too, the shallow lagoons, all ashy pale, crawling and shivering in the keen air, their little waves flying shoreward as if for shelter.

Out beyond San Giorgio, the fishing-boats are tethered to the spiles, their decks swept by fierce dashes of rain, their masts rocking wearily. Nearer in, this side the island, two gondolas with drenched *félzi*, manned by figures muffled in oilskins, fight every inch of the way to the Molo; they hug in mid stream the big P. and O. steamer lying sullen and deserted, her landing-ladder hanging useless, the puffs of white steam beaten flat against her red smoke-

146

stacks. Across the deserted canal the domes of
the Salute glisten like burnished silver in the
white light of the gale, and beyond these, tat-
ters of gray cloud-rack scud in from the sea.
Along the quays of the Dogana the stevedores
huddle in groups beneath the sheltering arches,
watching the half loaded boats surge and jar in
the ground-swell of the incoming sea. In the
garden at your very feet lie the bruised blossoms
of the oleanders, their storm-beaten branches
hanging over the wall, fagged out with the
battle of the night. Even the drenched tables
under the dripping arbors are strewn with wind-
swept leaves, and the overturned chairs are
splashed with sand.

All the light, all the color, all the rest and
charm and loveliness of Venice are dead. All
the tea-rose, sun-warmed marble, all the soft
purples of shifting shadows, all the pearly light
of summer cloud and the silver shimmer of
the ever-changing, million-tinted sea are gone.
Only cold, gray stone and dull, yellow water,
reflecting leaden skies, and black-stained columns, and water-soaked steps! Only brown
sails, wet, colorless gondolas, and disheartened,
baffled pigeons! To-day the wind blows east!

When the tide turns flood, the waters of the
lagoon, driven by the high wind, begin to rise.

Up along the Molo, where the gondolas land
their passengers, the gondoliers have taken
away their wooden steps. Now the sea is level
with the top stone of the pavement, and there
are yet two hours to high water. All about
the caffès under the Library, the men stand in
groups, sheltered from the driving rain by the
heavy canvas awnings laid flat against the door
columns. Every few minutes some one consults his watch, peering anxiously out to sea. A
waiter serving coffee says, in an undertone,
that it is twelve years since the women went
to San Marco in boats ; then the water rose to
the sacristy floor.

Under the arcades and between the columns
of the Doges' Palace is packed a dense mass of
people, watching the angry, lawless sea. Wagers
are freely laid that unless the wind shifts the
church itself will be flooded at high water. The
gondoliers are making fast their unused *félzi*,
lashing them to the iron lamp-posts. Along the
Molo the boats themselves, lashed fore and aft
to the slender poles, are rocking restlessly to
and fro.

Suddenly a loud cheer breaks from the throng
nearest the water's edge, and a great, surging
wave dashes across the flat stone and spreads
quickly in widening circles of yellow foam over

the marble flagging of the Piazzetta. Then another and another, bubbling between the iron tables and chairs of the caffès, swashing around the bases of the columns, and so on like a mill-race, up and around the Loggietta of the Campanile, and on into the Piazza with a rush. A wild shout goes up from the caffès and arcades. The waiters run quickly hither and thither, heaping up the chairs and tables. The shop-men are closing their shutters and catching up their goods. The windows of the Procuratie are filled with faces overjoyed at the sight. Troops of boys, breechless almost to their suspender buttons, are splashing about in glee. The sea is on the rampage. The bridegroom is in search of the bride. This time the Adriatic has come to wed the city. Another hour with the wind east, and only the altar steps of San Marco will suffice for the ceremony!

Another shout comes from the Piazzetta. There is a great waving of hands and hats. Windows are thrown open everywhere. The pigeons sweep in circles ; never in the memory of their oldest inhabitant has there been such a sight. In the excitement of the hour a crippled beggar slips from a bench and is half drowned on the sidewalk.

Another and a louder roar, and a gondola

rowed by a man in tarpaulins floats past the
Campanile, moves majestically up the flood,
and grounds on the lower steps of San Marco.
The boys plunge in and push, the women laugh
and clap their hands.

From the steps of the arcade of the Library,
men with bared thighs are carrying the shop-
girls to the entrance of the Merceria under the
clock tower. Some of the women are venturing
alone, their shoes and stockings held above their
heads. Farther down, near the corner column
of the Doges' Palace, a big woman, her feet
and ankles straight out, is breaking the back of
a little man who struggles along hip deep, followed by the laughter of the whole Piazzetta.

In the *campo* fronting the church of San Moisè,
a little square hemmed around by high buildings, the sea, having overflowed the sewers, is
spurting small geysers through the cracks in
the pavement, thumping and pounding a nest
of gondolas moored under the bridge.

Out on the Piazzetta a group of men, bare-
legged and bareheaded, are constructing a
wooden bridge from the higher steps of the arcade of the Library to the equally high steps
surrounding the base of the column of Saint
Theodore, and so on to the corner column of
the Doges' Palace. They are led by a young

fellow wearing a discarded fatigue cap, his trousers tied around his ankles. The only dry spot about him is the lighted end of a cigarette. This is Vittorio — up from the Via Garibaldi — out on a lark. He and his fellows — Luigi and the rest — have splashed along the Riva with all the gusto of a pack of boys revelling in an October snow. They have been soaking wet since daylight, and propose to remain so until it stops raining. The building of the bridge was an inspiration of Vittorio, and in five minutes every loose plank about the *traghetto* is caught up and thrown together, until a perilous staging is erected. Upon this Luigi dances and pirouettes to prove its absolute stability. When it topples over with the second passenger, carrying with it a fat priest in purple robe and shovel hat, who is late for the service and must reach the Riva, Luigi roars with laughter, stands his Reverence on his feet, and, before he can protest, has hoisted him aback and plunged knee deep into the flood.

The crowd yell and cheer, Vittorio holding his sides with laughter, until the dry flagging of the palace opposite is reached, and the reverend gentleman, all smiles and benedictions, glides like a turtle down Luigi's back.

But the tramps from the Via Garibaldi are not

satisfied. Luigi and Vittorio and little stumpy Appo, who can carry a sack of salt as easily as a pail of water, now fall into line, offering their broad backs for other passengers, Vittorio taking up a collection in his hat, the others wading about, pouncing down upon derelict oars, barrels, bits of plank, and the débris of the wrecked bridge. When no more *soldi* for ferry tolls are forthcoming, and no more Venetians, male or female, can be found reckless or hurried enough to intrust their precious bodies to Luigi's shoulders, the gang falls to work on a fresh bridge. This Vittorio has discovered hidden away in the recesses of the Library cellars, where it has lain since the last time the Old Man of the Sea came bounding over the Molo wall. There are saw-horses for support, and long planks with rusty irons fastened to each end, and braces, and cross-pieces. All these are put up, and the bridge made entirely practicable, within half an hour. Then the people cross and recross, while the silent gendarmes look on with good-natured and lazy indifference. One very grateful passenger drops a few *soldi* into Vittorio's water-soaked fatigue cap. Another, less generous, pushes him to one side, crowding some luckless fellow, who jumps overboard up to his knees to save himself from total immersion, the girls screaming with assumed fright, Vittorio coaxing and pleading, and Luigi laughing louder than ever.

At this moment a steamboat from the Lido attempts to make fast to her wharf, some hundreds of feet down the Molo. As the landing-planks are afloat and the whole dock awash, the women and children under the awnings of the after deck, although within ten feet of the solid stone wall, are as much at sea as if they were off the Lido. Vittorio and his mates take in the situation at a glance, and are alongside in an instant. Within five minutes a plank is lashed to a wharf-pile, a rope bridge is constructed, and Vittorio begins passing the children along, one by one, dropping them over Luigi's shoulders, who stands knee-deep on the dock. Then the women are picked up bodily, the men follow astride the shoulders of the others, and the impatient boat moves off to her next landing-place up the Giudecca.

By this time hundreds of people from all over the city are pouring into the Piazza, despite the driving rain and gusts of wind. They move in a solid mass along the higher arcades of the Library and the Palace. They crawl upon the steps of the columns and the sockets of the flag-staffs; they cling to the rail and pavement of the Loggietta—wherever a footing can be gained above the water-line. To a Venetian nothing is so fascinating as a spectacle of any kind, but it has been many a day since the Old Man of the Sea played the principal rôle himself !

There is no weeping or wailing about wet cellars and damp basements, no anxiety over damaged furniture and water-soaked carpets. All Venetian basements are damp ; it is their normal condition. If the water runs in, it will run out again. They have known this Old Sea King for centuries, and they know every whim in his head. As long as the Murazzi hold — the great stone dykes breasting the Adriatic out-side the lagoons — Venice is safe. To-morrow the blessed sun will shine again, and the warm air will dry up the last vestige of the night's frolic.

Suddenly the wind changes. The rain ceases. Light is breaking in the west. The weather-vane on the Campanile glows and flashes. Now a flood of sunshine bursts forth from a halo of lemon-colored sky. The joyous pigeons glint like flakes of gold. Then a shout comes from the Molo. The sea is falling ! The gondolier who has dared the centre of the Piazza springs to his oar, strips off his oilskins, throws them into his boat, and plunges overboard waist deep, seizing his gondola by the bow. The boys dash in on either side. Now for the Molo ! The crowd breaks into cheers. On it goes, grounding near the Porta della Carta, bumping over the stone flagging ; afloat again, the boatmen from the Molo leaping in to meet it ; then a rush, a cheer, and the endangered gondola clears the coping of the wall and is safe at her moorings.

Half an hour later the little children in their white summer dresses, the warm sunshine in their faces, are playing in the seaweed that strews the pavements of the Piazzetta.

LEGACIES OF THE PAST

WILL you have the kindness to present Professor Croisac's profound adoration to the Contessa Albrizzi, and say that he humbly begs permission to conduct his friend, a most distinguished painter, through the noble salons of her *palazzo?* "

It was the Professor, standing bareheaded on the landing-steps of the entrance to the Palazzo Albrizzi, the one lonely glove breaking the rounded outline of his well-brushed hat. He was talking to a portly Italian who did duty as Cerberus. As for myself, I was tucked back under the *tenda*, awaiting the result of the conference, Espero smiling at the old fellow's elaborate address and manners.

The porter bowed low, and explained, with much earnestness, that the *illustrissima* was then sojourning at her country seat in the Tyrol ; adding that, despite this fact, the whole palace, including the garden and its connecting bridge, from the courtyard to the roof, was completely at the service of the *Signor Professore.*

" And all for two *lire*," whispered Espero, to whom the old gentleman was a constant source of amusement, and who could never quite understand why most of his talking was done with his back bent at right angles to his slender legs. So we followed the porter up the stone staircase, around its many turns, to the grand hall above, with its rich pictures panelled on the walls, and so on through the various rooms of white stucco and old gold brocades, to the grand salon, the one with the famous ceiling.

The night before, over a glass of Torino vermouth at Florian's, the Professor had insisted that I should not live another day until he had piloted me through all those relics of the past, illustrative of an age in Venice as sumptuous as it was artistic.

First of all I must see the gorgeous ceiling of the Albrizzi ; then the curious vine-covered bridge leading out of the Contessa's boudoir to a garden across the narrow canal, as secluded as the groves of Eden before Adam stepped into them. Then I must examine the grand Palazzo Rezzonico, begun by Longhena in 1680 and completed sixty years later by Massari, once the home of Pope Clement XIII. and again made immortal as sheltering the room in which Browning had breathed his last. There, too, was the Barbaro, with its great flight of stone steps sweeping up and around two sides of a court to the picturesque entrance on the second floor, — the Barbaro, with its exquisite salon, by far the most beautiful in Europe. There was the Palazzo Pisani, built in the fifteenth century, its galleries still hung with Venetian mirrors; and the Palazzo Pesaro, designed by this same Longhena in 1679, the home of an illustrious line of Venetian nobles from Leonardo Pesaro down to the Doge Giovanni, with its uncanny row of grotesque heads of boars, bulls, and curious beasts studded along the water-table of the first story, a hand's touch from your gondola, so grotesque and quaint that each one looked like a nightmare solidified into stone. There were also the Dandolo, where lived the great Doge Enrico Dandolo, the conqueror of Constantinople, — conqueror at ninety-seven years of age; the Farsetti, where Canova studied, in his time an academy; the Barbarigo, where Titian once held court; the Mocenigo, where Byron lived; not to mention the veritable home of the veritable Desdemona, including the identical balcony where Othello breathed his love.

All these I must see, and more, — more in out-of-the-way churches like San Giorgio della Schiavoni, with the Carpaccios that are still as brilliant as when the great painter laid down his brush. More in the Gesuati up the Zattere, with its exquisite Tiepolos. Infinitely more in the school of San Rocco, especially behind the altars and under the choir-loft ; in the Frari next door, and in a dozen other picturesque churches ; and away out to Torcello, the mother of Venice, with its one temple, — the earliest of Venetian cathedrals, — its theatre-like rows of seats, and the ancient slate shutters swinging on huge hinges of stone.

But to return to the Professor, who is still gazing up into the exquisite ceiling of the salon of the Contessa, pointing out to me the boldness and beauty of the design, a white sheet drawn taut at the four corners by four heroic nude figures, its drooping folds patted up against the ceiling proper by a flutter of life-sized, winged cupids flying in the air, in high relief, or half smothered in its folds.

" Nothing gives you so clear an idea of the lives these great nobles lived," said the Professor, " as your touching something they touched, walking through their homes — the homes they lived in — and examining inch by inch the things they lived with. Now this Palazzo Albrizzi is perhaps less spacious and less costly than many others of the period ; but for all that, look at the grand hall, with its sides a continuous line of pictures, its ceiling a marvel of stucco and rich-colored canvases ! Do you find anything like this outside of Venice ? And now come through the salon, all white and gold, to the bridge spanning the canal. Here, you see, is where my lady steps across and so down into her garden when she would be alone. You must admit that this is quite unique.''

The Professor was right. A bridge from a boudoir to a garden wall, sixty or more feet above the water-line, is unusual, even in Venice.

And such a bridge ! All smothered in vines, threading their way in and out the iron lattice-work of the construction, and sending their tendrils swinging, heads down, like acrobats, to the water below. And such a garden ! Framed in by high prison walls, their tops patrolled by sentinels of stealthy creepers and wide-eyed morning-glories ! A garden with a little glass-covered arbor in the centre plot, holding a tiny figure of the Virgin ; circular stones benches for two, *and no more;* tree-trunks twisted into seats, with encircling branches for shoulders and back, and all, too, a thousand miles in the wilderness for anything you could hear or see of the life of the great city about you. A garden for lovers and intrigues and secret plots, and muffled figures smuggled through mysterious water-gates, and stolen whisperings in the soft summer night. A garden so utterly shut in — and so entirely shut out — that the daughter of a Doge could take her morning bath in the fountain with all the privacy of a boudoir.

"Yes," said the Professor, with a slight twinkle in his eye, "these old Venetians knew; and perhaps some of the modern ones."

And so we spent the day, rambling in and out of a dozen or more of these legacies of the past, climbing up wide palatial staircases; some still inhabited by the descendants of the noble families; others encumbered with new and old furniture, packing-boxes and loose straw, now magazines for goods; gazing up at the matchless equestrian statue of Colleoni, the most beautiful the world over; rambling through the San Giovanni e Paolo; stopping here and there to sketch, perhaps the Madonna over the gate next the Rezzonico, or some sculptured lion surmounting the newel-post of a still more ancient staircase; prying into back courts or up crumbling staircases, or opening dust-begrimed windows only to step out upon unkept balconies overhanging abandoned gardens; every carving, pillar, and rafter but so much testimony to the wealth, power, and magnificence of these rulers of the earth.

" And now to the Caffè Calcina for luncheon, Espero."

When we had dodged into its open door out of the heat, and were seated at one of its little square tables under the grapevines, the Professor fished up two books from that capacious inside pocket of his, and with much explanatory preface of how he had searched through all the book-stalls of the Rialto, finding them at last in the great library of the Doge's Palace itself, wiped their faded covers with a napkin, and turned the leaves tenderly with his withered fingers.

" And just see what festivities went on in these great palaces! Here is a little book written by Giustina Renier Michiel, and published early in the century. It is especially interesting as throwing some light on the wonderful festivities of the olden time. You remember the Palazzo Nani, the palace we saw after leaving the Dandolo? Well, listen to this account of a wonderful *fête* given in the beginning of the last century at this very palace." The Professor had closed the book over his finger, — he knew the description by heart.

"Michiel says that owing to the intense cold the lagoon was frozen over as far as Mestre, so the hospitable host warmed every part of the palace with huge stoves made of solid silver, elaborately wrought in exquisite designs ; and not content with the sum of that outlay, he completed the appointments and decorations in the same precious metal, even to the great candelabra lighting the entrance hall. And then, as a mere freak of hospitality, — he had a large visiting list, you may be sure, — he added ten rooms to his varied suites, in each one of which he placed musicians of different nationalities, just to prevent crowding, you see.

"And now let me read you of another. Part of the palace referred to here," he added, "has, I believe, been destroyed these many years. It was the home of Patrizio Grimani, — the palace where we saw the fine portrait of a Doge hanging near the window. That must have been the room in which the banquet took place. The stage referred to must have been erected in the room opening out from it. The author Michiel says, in describing a princely *fête* that took place here, that 'after the play' — performed by his private company in his own thea-

tre, remember — 'the guests were ushered into
an adjoining room and the doors closed. In half
an hour the doors were re-opened, discovering
a superb ballroom, with every vestige of the
theatre and its appointments swept away.'

"All years and years ago, *mon ami*," continued the Professor, closing the book, "and in
the very room that you and I walked through !
Think of the balconies crowded with Venetian
beauties in the richest of brocades and jewels !
Imagine that same old ruin of a garden, roofed
over and brilliant with a thousand lanterns ! See
the canals packed with gondolas, the torch-
bearers lighting the way ! Bah ! When I think
of the flare of modern gas-jets along the Champs
Elysées, and the crush of *fiacres* and carriages,
all held in check by a score of gendarmes in
black coats ; of the stuffy rooms and screeching
violins ; and then drink in the memory of these
fêtes, with their sumptuousness and grandeur,
I can hardly restrain my disgust for the cheap
shams of our times.

"And here is another ancient chronicle of
quite a different kind," opening the other book.
"You will find it more or less difficult, for it is
in old Italian, and some of its sentences, even
with my knowledge of the language," — this
with a certain wave of the hand, as if no one

had ever disputed it, — "I can only guess at. This, too, came from the library in the Doge's Palace, and is especially valuable as showing how little change there is between the Venice of to-day and the Venice of a century and a half ago, so far as localities and old landmarks go. The customs, I am delighted to say, have somewhat improved. It was written by one Edmondo Lundy in 1750.[1] He evidently came down to Venice to try his wings, and from his notes I should say he spread them to some purpose. He first fell into the clutches of a grand dame, — a certain noble lady, a Duchessa, — who sent for him the day after he arrived, and who complimented him upon his bearing and personal attractions. Then she explained that all Venetian ladies of position had attached to their persons a gentleman in waiting, a sort of *valet de place* of the heart, as it were, who made love to them in a kind of lute and guitar fashion, with ditties and song; that she had seen him on the Riva the afternoon before, had admired his figure and face, and being at the moment without any such attendant herself had determined to offer him the situation. His being a foreigner only increased her ardor, foreigners being at a high premium for such positions in

[1] *Misteri di Venezia*, di Edmondo Lundy.

165

those days. Although the Duchessa had already a husband of her own, was wrinkled, partly bald, and over sixty, Lundy, the gay cavalier, fell into the scheme. It is delightful to hear him tell of how the strange courtship progressed, one incident in particular : It was the custom of the fashionable set of the day to drift out in their gondolas up the Giudecca in the twilight, right in front of where we now sit ; you can see the spot from this window. Here they would anchor in mid stream and listen to recitals of music and poetry by some of the more gifted cavaliers, — lines from Dante and Tasso, — the servants and gondoliers serving the ices, which were all brought from this very Caffè Calcina. See, the name was spelled the same way. Does it not make you feel, as you sit here, that you have only to shut your eyes to bring it all back ? Oh, the grand days of the Republic ! These old vines above our heads could tell a story !

" But it seems that even the Duchessa palled on so versatile a cavalier as Lundy. She really bored him to death, so he hunts out a friend, explains the situation, and begs that he will get him out of the scrape. The friend writes a letter to Milan, and has it redelivered to Lundy, summoning him instantly to the bedside of a dying relative. This letter is shown to the

Duchessa, who parts with him with many tears and protestations, and Lundy leaves Venice. In three months he returns, hoping that some other equally handsome and attractive young foreigner has taken his place. Alas ! the black drapings of the Duchessa's gondola announce her death. And now comes the most comical part of it all. In her will she left him a thousand *lire* to purchase some souvenir expressive of the love and devotion with which he had inspired her !

" Further on Lundy tells how he watched for hours the efforts of two priests to get a break-fast. They were strung halfway up the Campanile, suspended outside the tower, between heaven and earth, in an iron cage. That, it seems, was the punishment inflicted on such unworthy gentlemen of the Church. They were considered to be better equipped than their parishioners to resist temptation, and so when they went astray they were strung up, like birds, in a cage. The only way these Lotharios got anything to eat was by letting down a string, to which some charitable soul would tie a flagon of wine or a loaf of bread. This morning the string was too short, and Lundy had no end of fun watching their efforts to piece it out with rosaries and sandal-lacings.

"Another time he was stopped by a poet on the Piazza, right in front of where Florian's now stands ; the same caffè, perhaps, who knows ? In those days, quite as it is now, the Piazza was a rendezvous for all Venice. All the doctors went there in search of patients, soliciting their patronage and holding out their diplomas. The mountebanks had performances on a carpet stretched on the pavement, and the actors played their parts in little booths erected between the clock tower and the Loggietta of the Campanile, — the roars of applause could be heard away out on the lagoons. The professional poets, too, would hand you copies of their latest productions, and buttonhole you long enough to have you listen to a sample stanza.

"Lundy was beguiled in this way, and an hour later discovered that his tobacco box, containing a portrait of his mother, set in brilliants — an old-fashioned snuff-box, perhaps — was missing. So, under the advice of a friend, he went to the headquarters of the city guard.

"'Where did you lose it ? ' said the Chief. 'Ah ! the poet. Do not worry. In two days please come again.'

"When he returned, the Chief said, —

"'Please take some tobacco.' It was from his own box!

"Then the Chief explained that in addition to being a poet, the man was also a member of the Borsaiuoli (literally translated, 'the takers'), from which our own word ' Bourse ' is derived.

"The same old swindlers still, only our stock-brokers do not stop at our tobacco boxes," added the Professor, laughing.

"Then Lundy goes on to explain that whatever these fellows succeeded in stealing they must bring to the Chief's office within three days. If the article was reclaimed within fifteen days, the thief received only a small sum, and the article was returned to its owner. If it was never called for, then it belonged to the thief. If he was detected in the act, or failed to return it to the office, he was punished.

" ' But why do you permit this ? ' continues Lundy, speaking to the Chief.

" ' To encourage an *ingenious, intelligent, sagacious activity among the people,*' replied the officer with perfect seriousness.

"See, I translate literally," said the Professor, with his finger on the line, throwing back his head in laughter.

But the day was not over for the Professor. We must go to the church of the Frari, the Professor going into raptures over the joyous Madonna and Saints by Bellini, while I had a little rapture of my own over a live, kneeling mother, illumined by a shaft of light which fell on her babe clasped to her breast, — a Madonna of to-day, infinitely more precious and lovely than any canvas which ages had toned to a dull smokiness. But then the Professor lives in the past, while I have a certain indefensible adoration for the present — when it comes to Madonnas.

Later we idled along between the columns supporting the roof, and wandered up behind the altar, the whole interior aglow with the afternoon sun, stopping at the monument of the great Titian and the tomb of Canova. To his credit be it said, the Professor had no raptures over this outrage in marble. And around all the other stone sepulchres of Doge, ambassador, and noble, lingering in the open door for a last glance back into its rich interior — certainly, after San Marco, the most picturesque and harmonious in coloring of all the churches in Venice — until we emerged into the sunlight and lost ourselves in the throngs of people blocking up the Campo. Then we turned the corner and entered San Rocco.

It was the *festa* day of the Frari, and the superb staircase of the Scuola di San Rocco, lined with the marvellous colorings of Titian and Tintoretto, was thronged with people in gala costume, crowding up the grand staircase to the upper *sala*, the room once used as an assembly room by the brotherhood of the order. I had seen it often before, without the Professor, for this was one of my many pilgrimages. Whenever you have an hour to spare, lose half your breath mounting this staircase. You will lose the other half when this magnificent council chamber bursts upon your view. Even the first sight of the floor will produce that effect.

You have doubtless, in your youth, seen a lady's brooch, fashionable then, made of Florentine mosaic, — a cunning, intricate joining of many-colored stones, — or perhaps a paperweight, of similar intricate design, all curves and scrolls. Imagine this paperweight, with its delicacy of fitting, high polish, and harmony of color, enlarged to a floor several hundred feet long, by a proportionate width, — I have not the exact dimensions, and it would convey no better idea if I had, — and you will get some faint impression of the quality and beauty of the floor of this grand *sala*. Rising from its polished surface and running halfway up the four walls, broken only by the round door you entered, with the usual windows and a corner chapel, is a wainscoting of dark wood carved in

171

alto relievo, in the last century, by Marchioni and his pupils. Above this is a procession of pictures, harmonizing in tone with the carvings and mosaics, and over all hangs a scroll-like ceiling incrusted with gold, its seven panels made luminous by Tintoretto's brush.

These panels are not his masterpieces. The side walls are equally unimportant, so far as the ravings of experts and art critics go. Even the carvings, on close inspection, are labored, and often grotesque. But to the painter's eye and mind this single *sala* of San Rocco, contrasted with all the other stately banquet halls and council chambers of Europe, makes of them but shelters to keep out the weather.

Filled with peasants and gala people in brilliant costumes on some *festa* day, when all may enter, the staircase crowded, its spacious interior a mass of colored handkerchief, shawl, and skirt, all flooded with the golden radiance of the sun, it is one of the rare sights of Venice. But even empty, with only your footfall and that of the bareheaded custodian to break the profound stillness, it is still your own ideal princely hall, — that hall where the most gallant knight of the most entrancing romance of your childhood could tread a measure with the fairest ladye of the loftiest, cragged-stepped castle ; that salon where the greatest nobles of your teeming fancy could strut about in ermine and cloth of gold ; where the wonderful knights held high revel, with goblets of crystal and flagons of ruby wine, and all the potentates from the spice-laden isles could be welcomed with trumpet and cymbal. Here you are sure Desdemona might have danced, and Katharine ; and here Cornaro, Queen of Cyprus, received the ambassadors of her promised kingdom. As you stand breathless, drinking in its proportions, you feel that it is a *sala* for pomps and ceremonies, not for monkish rites ; a *sala* for wedding breakfasts and gay routs and frolicsome masquerades and bright laughter, rather than for whispered conferences in cowl and frock. Even its polished floor recalls more readily the whirl of flying slippers than the slow, measured tread of sandalled feet.

The Professor himself, I regret to say, was not wildly enthusiastic over this interior. In fact, he made no remark whatever, except that the floor was too slippery to walk upon, and looked too *new* to him. This showed the keynote of his mind : the floor was laid within a century of the preceding generation. Nothing less than two centuries old ever interests the Professor !

However, despite his peculiarities, it is de-lightful to go about with the old fellow, listen-ing to his legends. Almost every palace and bridge stirs into life some memory of the past.

"Here," he says, "was where the great Doge Foscari lived, and from that very balcony were hung his colors the day of his abdication, — the colors that four hours later were draped in black at his tragic death. On that identical doorstep landed the ex-queen of Cyprus on the event-ful morning when she returned to Venice an exile in her own land." And did I know that on this very bridge — the Ponte dei Pugni, the bridge of the fisticuffs — many of the fights took place between the two factions of the gon-doliers, the Nicoletti and the Castellani? If I would leave the gondola for a moment he would show me the four impressions of the human foot set into the marble of the two upper steps, two on each side. Here each faction would place its two best men, their right feet cover-ing the stone outline ; then at a given signal the rush began. For days these fights would go on, and the canal be piled up with those thrown over the railless bridge. Soon the whole neigh-borhood would take sides, fighting on every street and every corner ; and once, so great was the slaughter, the tumult could be quelled only by the archbishop bringing out the Host from the church of Santa Barnaba, not far off, thus compelling the people to kneel.

When the day was over and we were floating through the little canal of San Trovaso, passing the great Palazzo Contarini, brilliant in the summer sunset, the Professor stopped the gondola and bade me good-by, with this parting comment : —

"It was either in this palace, in that room you see halfway up the wall, where the pointed Gothic windows look out into the garden, or perhaps in one of the palaces of the Procuratie, I forget which, that the King of Denmark, during the great *fêtes* attendant upon his visit in 1708, trod a measure with a certain noble dame of marvellous beauty, one Catarina Quirini, the wife of a distinguished Venetian. As he wheeled in the dance his buckle tore a string of priceless pearls from her dress. Before the King could stoop to hand them to his fair partner, her husband sprang forward and crushed them with his foot, remarking, 'The King never kneels.' Charming, was it not ? "

"What do you think it cost his Highness the next day, Professor ?" I asked.

"I never heard," he replied, with a shrug of his shoulders; " but what did it matter ? What are kings for ?"

" Good-night ! "

LIFE IN THE STREETS

THE gondola, like all other cabs, land or water, whether hansom, four-wheeler, sampan, or caïque, is a luxury used only by the hurried and the rich. As no Venetian is ever hurried, and few are rich, — very many of them living in complete ignorance of the exact whereabouts of their next repast, — almost everybody walks.

And the walking, strange to say, in this city anchored miles out at sea, with nearly every street paved with ripples, is particularly good. Of course one must know the way, — the way out of the broad Campo, down the narrow slit of a street between tall houses ; the way over the slender bridges, along stone foot-walks, hardly a yard wide, bracketed to some palace wall overhanging the water, or the way down a flight of steps dipping into a doorway and so under and through a greater house held up by stone columns, and on into the open again.

But when you do know all these twists and turns and crookednesses, you are surprised to find that you can walk all over Venice and never wet the sole of your shoe, nor even soil it, for that matter.

If you stand on the Iron Bridge spanning the Grand Canal, — the only dry-shod connection between the new part of Venice which lies along the Zattere, and the old section about San Marco and the Piazza, — you will find it crowded all day with hundreds of pedestrians passing to and fro. Some of them have come from away down near the Arsenal, walked the whole length of the Riva, rounded the Campanile, crossed the Piazza, and then twisted themselves through a tangle of these same little byways and about church corners and down dark cellars, — *sotto portico*, the street labels read, until they have reached the *campo* of San Stefano and the Iron Bridge. And it is so, too, at the Rialto, the only other bridge, but one, crossing the Grand Canal, except that the stream of idlers has here a different current, and poorer clothes are seen. Many of these streets are wide enough for a company of soldiers to walk abreast, and many are so narrow that when two fruit-venders pass with their baskets, one of them steps into a doorway.

And the people one meets in these twists and turns, — the people who live in the big and little streets, — who eat, sleep, and are merry, and who, in the warm summer days and nights, seem to have no other homes ! My dear friend Luigi is one of these vagrant Bohemians, and so is Vittorio, and little Appo, with shoulders like a stone Hercules and quite as hard, and so, also, are Antonio and the rest. When Luigi wants his breakfast he eats it from a scrap of paper held on the palm of his hand, upon which is puddled and heaped a little mound of thick soup or brown *ragout* made of *fulpe,* or perhaps shreds of fish. He will eat this as he walks, stopping to talk to every fellow tramp he meets, each one of whom dips in his thumb and forefinger with a pinch-of-snuff movement quite in keeping with the ancient custom and equally as courteous. Every other poverty-stricken *cavalière* of the Riva, as soon as he has loaded down his own palm with a similar greasy mess from the earthen dish simmering over a charcoal fire, — the open-air caffè of the poor, — expects that the next friend passing will do the same. When night comes they each select some particularly soft slab of marble on one of the seats in the shadow of the Campanile, or some bricked recess behind San Marco, stuff their hats under their cheeks, and drop into oblivion, only waking to life when the sun touches the gilded angel of San Giorgio. And not only Luigi and his fellow tramps, — delightful fellows every one of them, and dear particular friends of mine, — but hundreds of others of every class and condition of royal, irredeemable, irresponsible, never-ending poverty.

And as to making merry ! You should sit down somewhere and watch these millionaires of leisure kill the lazy, dreamy, happy-go-lucky hours with a volley of chaff hurled at some stroller, some novice from the country back of Mestre in for a day's holiday ; or with a combined good-natured taunt at a peasant from the fruit gardens of Malamocco, gaping at the wonders of the Piazza ; or in heated argument each with the other — argument ending only in cigarettes and *vino*. Or listen to their songs — songs started perhaps by some one roused out of a sound sleep, who stretches himself into shape with a burst of melody that runs like fire in tangled grass, until the whole Campo is ablaze: "Il Trovatore," and snatches from "Marta" and "Puritani," or some fisherman's chorus that the lagoons have listened to for centuries. You never hear any new songs. All the operas of the outside world, German, French, and English, might be sung and played under their noses and into their ears for a lifetime, and they would have none of them.

Then the street venders ! The man who stops at some water-steps to wash and arrange on a flat basket the handful of little silver fish, which he sells for a copper coin no larger than one of their fins. And the candy man with teetering scales ; and the girl selling the bright red handkerchiefs, blue suspenders, gorgeous neckties, and pearl buttons strung on white cards.

And, too, the grave, dignified, utterly useless, and highly ornamental gendarmes always in pairs, — never stopping a moment, and always with the same mournful strut, — like dual clog-dancers stepping in unison. In many years' experience of Venetian life, I have never yet seen one of these silver-laced, cockaded, red-striped-pantalooned guardians of the peace lay his hand upon any mortal soul. Never, even at night, when the ragged wharf-rats from the shipyards prowl about the Piazza, sneaking under the tables, pouncing upon the burnt ends of cigarettes and cigars, and all in sight of these pillars of the state, — never, with all these opportunities, even when in their eagerness these ragamuffins crawl almost between their legs.

Yes, once ! Then I took a hand myself, and against the written law of Venice, too. It was at Florian's, on the very edge of the sea of tables, quite out to the promenade line. I was enjoying a glass of Hofbrau, the stars overhead, the music of the King's band filling the soft summer night. Suddenly a bust of Don Quixote, about the size of my beer-mug, was laid on the table before me, and a pair of black eyes from under a Spanish *boina* peered into my own.

" Cinque lire, signore."

It was Alessandro, the boy sculptor.

I had met him the day before, in front of Salviati's. He was carrying into the great glass-maker's shop, for shipment over the sea, a bust made of wet clay. A hurried sojourner, a foreigner, of course, by an awkward turn of his heel had upset the little sculptor, bust and all, pasting the aristocratic features of Don Quixote to the sidewalk in a way that made that work of art resemble more the droppings from a mortar hod than the counterfeit presentment of Cervantes' hero. Instantly a crowd gathered, and a commiserating one. When I drew near enough to see into the face of the boy, it was wreathed in a broad smile. He was squatting flat on the stone flagging, hard at work on the damaged bust, assuring the offending *signore* all the while that it was sheer nonsense

182

to make such profuse apologies, — it would be
all right in a few minutes; and while I looked
on, in all less than ten minutes, the deft fingers
of the little fellow had readjusted with marvellous dexterity the crumpled mass, straighten-
ing the neck, rebuilding the face, and restoring
the haughty dignity of the noble *don*. Then
he picked himself up, and with a bow and a
laugh went on his way rejoicing. A boy of any
other nationality, by the bye, would have filled
the air with his cries until a policeman had
taught him manners, or a hat lined with pennies had healed his sorrows.

So when Alessandro looked up into my face
I felt more like sharing my table with him than
driving him away — even to the ordering of another beer and a chair. Was he not a brother
artist, and though poor and with a very slender hold on fame and fortune, had art any di-
viding lines ?

Not so the gentlemen with the cocked hats !
What ! Peddling without the King's license, or
with it, for that matter, at Florian's, within
sound of the King's band, the eyes of all Venice upon them ! Never ! So they made a grab
for Alessandro, who turned his innocent young
face up into theirs, — he was only two days
from Milan and unused to their ways, — and,

finding that they were really in earnest, clung to me like a frightened kitten.

Of course it became instantly a matter of professional pride with me. Allow a sculptor of renown and parts, not to say genius, to be dragged off to prison under the pretence that he was breaking the law by selling his wares, when really he was only exhibiting to a brother artist an evidence of his handiwork, etc. ! It was a narrow escape, and I am afraid the by-standers, as well as the frozen images of the law, lost all respect for my truthfulness, — but it sufficed.

On my way home that night this waif of the streets told me that since he had been ten years old — he was then only seventeen — he had troubadoured it through Europe, even as far as Spain, his only support being his spatula and a lump of clay. With these he could conjure a breakfast out of the head waiter of a caffè in exchange for his portrait in clay, or a lodging in some cheap hotel for a like payment to the proprietor. He is still tramping the streets of Venice, his little wooden board filled with Ma-donnas, Spanish matadors, and Don Quixotes. Now he has money in the bank, and the striped-pantalooned guardians of the peace let him alone.

And the girls !

Not the better class, with mothers and duennas dogging every footstep, but the girls who wander two and two up and down the Riva, their arms intertwined; not forgetting the bright-eyed *signorina* that I once waylaid in a by-street. (Don't start; Espero helped!) I wanted a figure to lean over a crumbling wall in a half-finished sketch, and sent Espero to catch one. Such a vision of beauty! Such a wealth of purple — grape purple — black hair; such luminous black eyes, real gazelle's, soft and velvety; so exquisitely graceful; so charming and naïve; so unkempt, so ragged, — so entirely unlaundered, unscrubbed, and slovenly!

But you must look twice at a Venetian beauty. You may miss her good points otherwise. You think at first sight that she is only the last half of my description, until you follow the flowing lines under the cheap, shabby shawl and skirt, and study the face.

This one opened her big eyes wide in astonishment at Espero, listened attentively, consented gracefully, and then sprang after him into the gondola, which carried her off bodily to my sketching ground. Truly one touch of the brush, with a paper *lira* neatly folded around the handle, is very apt to make all Venice, especially stray amateur models, your kin.

But this is true of all the people in the streets. Every Venetian, for that matter, is a born model. You can call from under your umbrella to any passer-by, anybody who is not on a quick run for the doctor, and he or she will stand stock still and fix himself or herself in any position you may wish, and stay fixed by the hour.

And the gossip that goes on all day ! In the morning hours around the wells in the open Campo, where the women fill their copper wa-ter-buckets, and the children play by the widen-ing puddles ; in the narrow streets beside a shadow-flecked wall ; under the vines of the *traghetto*, lolling over the unused *félzi;* among the gondoliers at the gondola landings, while their boats lie waiting for patrons ; over low walls of narrow slits of canals, to occupants of some window or bridge a hundred feet away ! There is always time to talk, in Venice.

Then the *dolce far niente* air that pervades these streets ! Nobody in a hurry. Nobody breaking his neck to catch a boat off for the Lido ; there will be another in an hour, and if, by any combination of cool awnings, warm wine, and another idler for company, this later boat should get away without this one passen-ger, why worry ? — to-morrow will do.

All over Venice it is the same. The men sit

186

in rows on the stone benches. The girls idle in the doorways, their hands in their laps. The members of the Open-Air Club lounge over the bridges or lie sprawled on the shadow side of the steps. Up in the fishing quarter, between naps in his doorway, some weather-beaten old salt may perhaps have a sudden spasm of energy over a crab basket that must be hoisted up, or lowered down, or scrubbed with a broom. But there is sure to be a lull in his energy, and before you fairly miss his toiling figure he is asleep in his boat. When his *signora* wakes him into life again with a piece of toasted pumpkin, — his luncheon, like the Professor's, is eaten wherever he happens to be, — he may have another spasm of activity, but the chances are that he will relapse into oblivion again.

Even about the Piazza, the centre of the city's life, every free seat that is shady is occupied. So, too, are the bases of the flagpoles in front of the Loggietta and behind the Campanile. Only when something out of the common moves into the open space — like the painter with the canvas ten feet long and six feet high — do these *habitués* leave their seats or forsake the shelter of the arcades and stand in solemn circle. This particular painter occupies the centre of a square bounded by four chairs and some

187

yards of connecting white ribbon, — the chairs turned in so that nobody can sit on them. He has been here for many seasons. He comes every afternoon at five and paints for an hour. The crowds, too, come every day, — the same people, I think. Yet he is not the only painter in the streets. You will find them all over Venice. Some under their umbrellas, the more knowing under short gondola sails rigged like an awning, under which they crawl out of the blazing heat. I am one of the more knowing.

The average citizen, as I have said, almost always walks. When there are no bridges across the Grand Canal he must of course rely on the gondola. Not the luxurious gondola with curtains and silk-fringed cushions, but a gondola half worn out and now used as a ferry-boat at the *traghetto*. These shuttles of travel run back and forth all day and all night (there are over thirty *traghetti* in Venice), the fare being some infinitesimally small bit of copper. Once across, the Venetian goes on about his way, dry-shod again. For longer distances, say from the railroad station to the Piazza, the Public Garden, or the Lido, he boards one of the little steamers that scurry up and down the Grand Canal or the Giudecca and the waters of some of the lagoons — really the only energetic things in

Venice. Then another bit of copper coin, this time the size of a cuff-button, and he is whirled away and landed at the end of a dock lined with more seats for the weary, and every shaded space full.

Another feature of these streets is the bric-à-brac dealer. He has many of the characteristics of his equally shrewd brethren along Cheapside and the Bowery. One in particular, — he is always on the sidewalk in front of his shop. The Professor insists that these men are the curse of Venice ; that they rob poor and rich alike, — the poor of their heirlooms at one tenth their value, the rich of their gold by reselling this booty at twenty times its worth. I never take the Professor seriously about these things. His own personal patronage must be very limited, and I suspect, too, that in the earlier years of his exile, some of his own belongings — an old clock, perhaps, or a pair of paste buckles, or some other relic of better days — were saved from the pawnshop only to be swallowed up by some shark down a back street.

But there is one particular Ananias, a smug, persuasive, clean-shaven specimen of his craft, who really answers to the Professor's epithet. He haunts a narrow crack of a street leading from the Campo San Moisè to the Piazza. This

crevice of a lane is the main thoroughfare between the two great sections of Venice. Not
only the Venetians themselves, but, as it is
the short cut to San Marco, many of the strangers from the larger hotels — the Britannia, the
Grand, the Bauer-Grünwald, and others —
pass through it night and day.

Here this wily spider weaves his web for
foreign flies, retreating with his victim into his
hole — a little shop, dark as a pocket — whenever he has his fangs completely fastened upon
the fly's wallet. The bait is perhaps a church
lamp, or an altar-cloth spotted with candle-
grease. There are three metres in the cloth,
with six spots of grease to the metre. You are
a stranger and do not know that the silk factory
at the corner furnished the cloth the week before for five francs a metre, Ananias the grease,
and his wife the needle that sewed it together.
Now hear him !

" No, nod modern ; seexteenth century.
Vrom a vary olt church in Padua. Zat von you
saw on ze Beazzi yesterday vas modern and vary
often, but I assure you, shentleman, zat zees
ees antique and more seldom. Ant for dree hundredt francs eet ees re-diklous. I bay myselluf
dree hundredt an' feefty francs, only ze beesi-
ness is so bad, and eet ees de first dime zat I

speak wis you, I vould not sell eet for fife hundredt.''

You begin by offering him fifty francs.

'' *Two hundredt* and feefty francs ! '' he answers, without a muscle in his face changing.
'' No, shentleman, it vould be eemposseeble
to '' —

'' No, fifty,'' you cry out.

Now see the look of wounded pride that over-
spreads his face, the dazed, almost stunned expression, followed by a slight touch of indignation. '' Shentleman, conseeder ze honor of my
house. Eef I sharge you dree hundredt francs
for sometings only for feefty, it ees for myselluf
I am zorry. Eet ees not posseeble zat you know
ze honorable standing of my house.''

Then, if you are wise, you throw down your
card with the name of your hotel, and stroll
up the street, gazing into the shop windows and
pricing in a careless way every other thing suspended outside any other door, or puckered up
inside any other window.

In ten minutes after you have turned the corner he has interviewed the porter of your hotel
— not Joseph of the Britannia ; Joseph never
lets one of this kind mount the hotel steps unless his ticket is punched with your permission.
In five minutes Ananias has learned the very

hour of the day you have to leave Venice, and is thereafter familiar with every bundle of stuffs offered by any other dealer that is sent to your apartment. When you pass his shop the next day he bows with dignity, but never leaves his doorway. If you have the moral courage to ignore him, even up to the last morning of your departure, when your trunks are packed and under the porter's charge for registering, you will meet Ananias in the corridor with the altar-cloth under his arm, and his bill for fifty francs in his pocket. If not, and you really want his stuffs and he finds it out, then cable for a new letter of credit.

At night, especially *festa* nights, these Venetian streets are even more unique than in the day. There is perhaps a *festa* at the Frari, or at Santa Maria del Zobenigo. The *campo* in front of the church is ablaze with strings of lanterns hung over the heads of the people, or fastened to long brackets reaching out from the windows. There are clusters of candles, too, socketed in triangles of wood, and flaring torches, fastened to a mushroom growth of booths that have sprung up since morning, where are sold hot waffles cooked on open-air griddles, and ladles full of soup filled with sea horrors, — spider-like things with crawly legs. Each booth is decorated with huge brass plaques, *repoussé* in designs of the Lion of St. Mark, and of the Saint himself. The cook tells you that he helped hammer them into shape during the long nights of the preceding winter ; that there is nothing so beautiful, and that for a few *lire* you can add these specimens of domestic bric-à-brac to your collection at home. He is right ; hung against a bit of old tapestry, nothing is more decorative than one of these rude reproductions of the older Venetian brass. And nothing more *honest*. Every indentation shows the touch of the artist's hammer.

In honor of the *festa* everybody in the vicinity lends a hand to the decorations. On the walls of the houses fronting the small square, especially on the wall of the wine shop, are often hung the family portraits of some neighbor who has public spirit enough to add a touch of color to the general enjoyment. My friend Pasquale D' Este, who is *gastaldo* at the *traghetto* of Zobenigo, pointed out to me, on one of these nights, a portrait of his own ancestor, surprising me with the information that his predecessors had been gondoliers for two hundred years.

While the *festa* lasts the people surge back and forth, crowding about the booths, buying knickknacks at the portable shops. All are

193

good-natured and courteous, and each one delighted over a spectacle so simple and so crude ;
the wonder is, when one thinks how often a
festa occurs in Venice, that even a handful of
people can be gathered together to enjoy it.

Besides all these varying phases of street
merrymaking, there are always to be found in
the thoroughfares of Venice, during the year,
some outward indications that mark important
days in the almanac — calendar days that neither
celebrate historical events nor mark religious
festivals. You always know, for instance, when
St. Mark's day comes, in April, as every girl you
meet wears a rose tucked in her hair out of deference to the ancient custom, not as a sign of the
religious character of the day, but to show to the
passer-by that she has a sweetheart. Before
Christmas, too, if in the absence of holly berries
and greens you should have forgotten the calendar day, the pedler of eels and of nut candy
and apple sauce would remind you of it ; for in
accordance with the ancient custom, dating back
to the Republic, every family in Venice, rich or
poor, the night before Christmas, has the same
supper, — eels, a nut candy called *mandorlato*,
and a dish of apple sauce with fruits and mustard. This is why the pedlers in Venice are
calling out all day at the top of their lungs,

"Mandorlato! Mostarda!" while the eel and mustard trade springs into an activity unknown for a year. On other saints' days the street pedlers sell a red paste made of tomatoes and chestnut flour, moulded into cakes.

Last are the caffès! In winter, of course, the *habitués* of these Venetian lounging places are crowded into small, stuffy rooms; but in the warmer months everybody is in the street. Not only do Florian's and the more important caffès of the rich spread their cloths under the open sky, but every other caffè on the Riva — the Oriental, the Veneta Marina, and the rest — pushes its tables quite out to the danger line patrolled by the two cocked-hat guardians of the peace. In and out between these checkerboards of good cheer, the pedlers of sweets, candies, and fruit strung on broom-straws ply their trade, while the flower girls pin tuberoses or a bunch of carnations to your coat, and the ever-present and persistent guide waylays customers for the next day's sight-seeing. Once or twice a week there is also a band playing in front of one of these principal caffès, either the government band or some private orchestra.

On these nights the people come in from all over Venice, standing in a solid mass, — men, women, and children listening in perfect silence to the strains of music that float over the otherwise silent street. There is nothing in Europe quite like this bareheaded, attentive, absorbed crowd of Venetians, enjoying every note that falls on their ears. There is no gathering so silent, so orderly, so well bred. The jewelled occupants of many an opera-box could take lessons in good manners from these denizens of the tenements, — fishermen, bead-stringers, lacemakers, — who gather here from behind the Shipyard and in the tangle of streets below San Giorgio della Schiavoni. There is no jostling or pushing, with each one trying to get a better place. Many of the women carry their babies, the men caring for the larger children. All are judges of good music, and all are willing to stand perfectly still by the hour, so that they themselves may hear and let others hear too.

NIGHT IN VENICE

NIGHT in Venice ! A night of silver moons, — one hung against the velvet blue of the infinite, fathomless sky, the other at rest in the still sea below !

A night of ghostly gondolas, chasing specks of stars in dim canals; of soft melodies broken by softer laughter ; of tinkling mandolins, white shoulders, and telltale cigarettes. A night of gay lanterns lighting big barges, filled with singers and beset by shadowy boats, circling like moths or massed like water-beetles. A night when San Giorgio stands on tiptoe, Narcissus-like, to drink in his own beauty mirrored in the silent sea ; when the angel crowning the Campanile sleeps with folded wings, lost in the countless stars ; when the line of the city from across the wide lagoons is but a string of lights buoying golden chains that sink into the depths ; when the air is a breath of heaven, and every sound that vibrates across the never-ending wave is the music of another world.

No pen can give this beauty, no brush its color, no tongue its delight. It must be seen and felt. It matters little how dull your soul may be, how sluggish your imagination, how dead your enthusiasm, here Nature will touch you with a wand that will stir every blunted sensibility into life. Palaces and churches, — poems in stone, — canvases that radiate, sombre forests, oases of olive and palm, Beethoven, Milton, and even the great Michael himself, may have roused in you no quiver of delight nor thrill of feeling.

But here, — here by this wondrous city of the sea, here where the transcendent goddess of the night spreads her wings, radiant in the light of an August moon, her brow studded with stars, — even were your soul of clay, here would it vibrate to the dignity, the beauty, and the majesty of her matchless presence.

As you lie, adrift in your gondola, hung in mid air, — so like a mirror is the sea, so vast the vault above you, — how dreamlike the charm ! How exquisite the languor ! Now a burst of music from the far-off Plaza, dying into echoes about the walls of San Giorgio ; now the slow tolling of some bell from a distant tower ; now the ripple of a laugh, or a snatch of song, or the low cooing of a lover's voice, as a ghostly skiff with drawn curtains and muffled light glides past; and now the low plash of the rowers as some phantom ship looms above you with bow-lights aglow, crosses the highway of silver, and melts into shadow.

Suddenly from out the stillness there bursts across the bosom of the sleeping wave the dull boom of the evening gun, followed by the long blast of the bugle from the big warship near the Arsenal; and then, as you hold your breath, the clear, deep tones of the great bell of the Campanile strike the hour.

Now is the spell complete!

The Professor, in the seat beside me, turns his head, and with a cautioning hand to Espero to stay his oar, listens till each echo has had its say, — first San Giorgio's wall, then the Public Garden, and last the low murmur that pulsates back from the outlying islands of the lagoon. On nights like these the Professor rarely talks. He lies back on the yielding cushions, his eyes upturned to the stars, the glow of his cigarette lighting his face. Now and then he straightens himself, looks about him, and sinks back again on the cushions, muttering over and over again, "Never such a night — never, never!" To-morrow night he will tell you the same thing, and every other night while the moon lasts.

Yet he is no empty enthusiast. He is only en-
thralled by the splendor of his mistress, this
matchless Goddess of Air and Light and Melody. Analyze the feeling as you may, despise
its sentiment or decry it altogether, the fact remains, that once get this drug of Venice into
your veins, and you never recover. The same
thrill steals over you with every phase of her
wondrous charm, — in the early morning, in the
blinding glare of the noon, in the cool of the
fading day, in the tranquil watches of the night.
It is Venice the Beloved, and there is none
other!

Espero has breathed her air always, and hundreds of nights have come and gone for him;
yet as he stands bareheaded behind you, his oar
slowly moving, you can hear him communing
with himself as he whispers, "Bella notte, bella
notte," just as some other devotee would tell
his beads, in unconscious prayer. It is the spirit
of idolatry born of her never-ending beauty
that marks the marvellous power which Venice
wields over human hearts, compelling them, no
matter how dull and leaden, to reverence and to
love.

And the Venetians never forget! While we
float idly back to the city, the quays are
crowded with people, gazing across the wide

lagoons, drinking in their beauty, the silver moon over all. Now and then a figure will come down to the water's edge and sit upon some marble steps, gazing seaward. There is nothing to be seen, — no passing ship, no returning boat. It is only the night!

Away up the canal, Guglielmo, the famous singer, once a gondolier, is filling the night with music, a throng of boats almost bridging the canal, following him from place to place, Luigi, the primo, in the lead, — the occupants hanging on every note that falls from his lips.

Up the Zattere, near San Rosario, where the afternoon sun blazed but a few hours since, the people line the edge of the marble quay, their children about them, the soft radiance of the night glorifying the Giudecca. They are of all classes, high and low. They love their city, and every phase of her beauty is to them only a variation of her marvellous charm. The Grand Duchess of the Riva stands in the doorway of her caffè, or leans from her chamber window; Vittorio and little Appo, and every other member of the Open-Air Club, are sprawled over the Ponte Veneta Marina, and even the fishermen up the Pallada sit in front of their doors. Venice is decked out to-night in all the glory of an August moon. They must be there to see!

You motion to Espero, and with a twist of his blade he whirls the gondola back to the line of farthest lights. As you approach nearer, the big Trieste steamer looms above you, her decks crowded with travellers. Through her open portholes you catch the blaze of the electric lights, and note the tables spread and the open staterooms, the waiters and stewards moving within. About her landing-ladders is a swarm of gondolas bringing passengers, the porters taking up the trunks as each boat discharges in turn.

A moment more and you shoot alongside the Molo and the water-steps of the Piazzetta. An old man steadies your boat while you alight. You bid Espero good-night and mingle with the throng. What a transition from the stillness of the dark lagoon !

The open space is crowded with idlers walking in pairs or groups. The flambeaux of gas-jets are ablaze. From behind the towering Campanile in the great Piazza comes a burst of music from the King's Band. Farther down the Riva, beyond the Ponte Paglia, is heard the sound of another band. Everywhere are color and light and music. Everywhere stroll the happy, restful, contented people, intoxicated with the soft air, the melody, and the beauty of the night.

If you think you know San Marco, come stand beneath its rounded portals and look up. The deep coves, which in the daylight are lost in the shadows of the dominant sun, are now illumined by the glare of a hundred gas-jets from the street below. What you saw in the daylight is lost in the shadow, — the shadowed coves now brilliant in light. To your surprise, as you look, you find them filled with inscriptions and studded with jewels of mosaic, which flash and glint in the glare of the blazing flambeaux. All the pictures over the great doors now stand out in bold coloring, with each caramel of mosaic distinct and clear. Over every top-moulding you note little beads and dots of gray and black. If you look closer two beads will become one, and soon another will burst into wings. They are the countless pigeons roosting on the carving. They are out of your reach, some fifty feet above you, undisturbed by all this glitter and sound.

As you turn and face the great square of the Piazza, you find it crowded, to the very arcades under the surrounding palaces, with a moving mass of people, the tables of the caffès reaching almost to the band-stand placed in the middle. Florian's is full, hardly a seat to be had. Auguste and his men are bringing ices and cooling drinks. The old Duchess of uncertain age, with the pink veil, is in her accustomed seat, and so are the white-gloved officers with waxed mustaches, and the pretty Venetian girls with their mothers and duennas. The Professor drops into his seat against the stone pillar, — the seat covered with leather, — lights another cigarette, and makes a sign to Auguste. It is the same old order, a cup of coffee and the smallest drop of cognac that can be brought in a tear-bottle of a decanter the size of your thumb.

When the music is over you stroll along the arcades and under the Bocca del Leone, and through the narrow streets leading to the *campo* of San Moisè, and so over the bridge near the Bauer-Grünwald to the crack in the wall that leads you to the rear of your own quarter. Then you cross your garden and mount the steps to your rooms, and so out upon your balcony.

The canal is deserted. The music-boats have long since put out their lanterns and tied up for the night. The lighters at the Dogana opposite lie still and motionless, their crews asleep under the mats stretched on the decks. Away up in the blue swims the silver moon, attended by an escort of clouds hovering close about her. Towering above you rises the great dome of the

Salute, silent, majestic, every statue, cross, and scroll bathed in the glory of her light.

Suddenly, as you hang over your balcony, the soft night embracing you, the odor of oleanders filling the air, you hear the quick movement of a flute borne on the night wind from away up the Iron Bridge. Nearer it comes, nearer,— the clear, bird-like notes floating over the still canal and the deserted city. You lean forward and catch the spring and rhythm of the two gondoliers as they glide past, keeping time to the thrill of the melody. You catch, too, the abandon and charm of it all. He is standing over her, his head uncovered, the moonlight glinting on the uplifted reed at his lips. She lies on the cushions beneath him, throat and shoulders bare, a light scarf about her head. It is only a glimpse, but it lingers in your memory for years, —you on the balcony and alone.

Out they go, —out into the wide lagoon, — out into the soft night, under the glory of the radiant stars. Fainter and fainter falls the music, dimmer and dimmer pales the speck with its wake of silver.

Then all is still!

THE GOOD GRAY NUN

MY gondolier, Ingenio, is a wrinkled old sea-dog, with gray hair and stooping shoulders, who has the air of a retired buccaneer and the voice of a girl. His gondola has been my home for a month past, and he has been my constant companion. As he speaks nothing but Italian and I nothing resembling it, we have adopted a sign language which answers perfectly. This morning he comes through the garden where I am taking my coffee, points to his gondola floating at the foot of the marble steps leading to the Grand Canal, touches his forehead, then his pocket, holds up two fingers, and motions as if to sit down. I understand at once that he has thought of a new shop where for a few francs we can buy two antique chairs, of a pattern especially desired by me.

These chairs have greatly bothered Ingenio. Under the plea of searching for them, I have ransacked half the old palaces in Venice, and have discovered most marvellous rooms, with ceilings of carved beams edged with gilt, with faded frescoes, exquisite marble staircases leading thereto, and often quaint and picturesque interiors inhabited by the present generation.

I have, of course, found every variety of chair, old and new, but the search has been so delightful, and the discoveries have partaken so much of the unexpected, that I refuse to be satisfied with any of them, and so continue my explorations; Ingenio poking the nose of his gondola into every crooked canal in Venice, and I my own up one half of her equally crooked staircases and across many an old courtyard and damp, mould-covered garden.

But this morning I shook my head, which was full of another and a more brilliant idea, — an idea which I conveyed to Ingenio by pointing down the canal with my umbrella staff, putting up my hands like a little praying Samuel, and sketching an imaginary bridge on the tablecloth with my coffee spoon.

Ingenio understood at once. He knew that I wanted to paint the bridge near the old church on the Riva degli Schiavoni.

In five minutes we were floating past the Piazza and San Marco, and in as many more had reached the quay near the church of the Santa Maria della Pietà.

I had seen a group of fishing-boats moored

here as I drifted past the afternoon before, and I reasoned that, as the tide did not change until noon, there was perhaps time to catch them before they spread their gorgeous wings of red and gold, and flew away to their homes in Chioggia.

We landed at the small piazza which formed the quay, at the end of which ran a flight of marble steps up and over the bridge. To the left of this were moored the boats with all sails set, hanging listless in the still air. In front was the white marble pavement baking in the sun.

I soon found the open door of the Santa Maria was my only shelter from the blinding heat. By hugging one side of the porch, and resting one leg of my easel against the lower hinge, I was sheltered in the shadow, and could still see the subject of my picture entire. So without more ado, I opened my folding seat and unlimbered my trap, while Ingenio filled the water bottles.

There are so many white umbrellas and floating studios in Venice that an artist at work excites very little curiosity. Occasionally the novelty of my position would tempt some penitent to glance over my shoulder, as she entered the church, making room lest she disturb me, but with this exception I worked on without interruption.

208

As the heat increased, the worshippers grew less numerous and the quay became nearly deserted. Ingenio, who had gone to sleep in the shadow, was now broiling in the sun, and my left or palette hand felt scorching hot.

But these are trifles when you have two fishing-boats half finished, the tide to turn in two hours, and you begin to note the crew already moving about and restlessly handling the ropes. You grow nervous every time a man goes ashore, lest he shall cast off the moorings, and so wreck your morning's work.

Suddenly a sunbeam shot across the upper corner of my canvas. I looked around and up. The sun was slanting over and down the cornice of the church, and with such intensity that I felt an immediate change of base imperative. You cannot see color by the side of a sunbeam.

In Venice, when your best friends fail and life begins to be a burden, you have one resource, — you call for your gondolier. So I awoke Ingenio. He appreciated the situation at once. He ran to the gondola, brought back my large umbrella, and wasted ten minutes of my precious time in attempting to drive its spiked staff into a flight of polished marble steps. The only result was the loss of the spike and the little that remained of my good temper.

After this failure I decided that heroic treatment was all that was left. I first pointed to my half-finished sails, seized the ropes in an imaginary sort of way as if lowering them, and then lifted my hands in despair. Then I gave him two francs, and followed him with my eyes as he disappeared over the bridge and reappeared on the deck of one of the boats.

A row of grinning faces all looked my way, and in a moment more Ingenio returned without the money and with one of the fishermen. The latter gazed silently at my sketch and said, "Buono." I was reassured. The sails were safe, at all events. But the heat continued to be frightful.

Another pantomime then followed with Ingenio, to which the fisherman lent a helping hand. I unfolded my plan slowly and with some misgivings. Ingenio turned a trifle pale and the fisherman looked somewhat alarmed. Five francs more, and a pleasanter expression asserted itself in the latter's face. Then they both measured the distance between the two doors, found an iron hook high up on the mouldings over the arch, returned to the boats, and in five minutes I had rigged an orange-colored jib sail across the entrance of the church, and had crawled in underneath, out of the sun, into its grateful shadow !

I do not offer any apology for this. I distinctly vow that I intended no disrespect to the most holy Maria della Pietà. I was simply backed up into a church door on the sunny side of a quay, with the thermometer in the nineties, an unfinished sketch before me, a marble wall behind me, and but two hours of tide remaining. The effect of a jib sail on Venetian church architecture was not under consideration by me. The possible loss of one in my picture was at the moment of greater importance.

At that instant the horror-stricken and very oily face of a well-fed priest peered into my improvised tent, and from it followed a torrent of Italian. I raised my hat meekly, bowed reverently, and pointed to Ingenio. While the discussion lasted, I managed to finish the rigging, the awning on deck, and the gondola alongside, but the crisis had arrived. I must either take in the jib or go with the priest. This sentiment seemed also to be shared by the crowd. I preferred the latter, and detailing the fisherman to stand by and "repel boarders," I called Ingenio, and followed his oiliness through the cool church, down a long passage, and up to a dark green door heavily hinged and locked.

The priest touched a bell, footsteps were heard, and a sliding panel revealed the sad face of a nun. A word of explanation followed, the bolts were shot back, and I found myself in a small vestibule leading into a low room, white, bare, and scrupulously clean. In a moment more the nun returned, bringing the Mother Superior. I saluted her as if she had been the Queen of Sheba. She listened incredulously to the voluble priest as he elaborated the outrage, and then indignantly turned to Ingenio, who hung his head and chewed the rim of his hat. Then she raised both hands as if in amazement, looked me straight in the face, and slowly shook her head. The sad-faced nun waited, and heard me expostulate in my choicest English that I had the greatest reverence for every church in Italy and for every Lady Superior. I only objected to the climate, and to the fact that this particular church was not on the shady side of the quay.

Then the nun slipped away, and presently returned with a sister in gray, who had the face of a Madonna and the voice of an angel, and an English angel at that. She questioned the priest, then Ingenio, then the sad-faced nun, and then turned to me.

Did the painter speak Italian ? Not a word. Furthermore, he was a stranger in a foreign land, away from the home of his childhood, without friends except this poor gondolier, his only possession being a half-finished sketch and a jib sail, for both of which he pleaded.

She listened, half smiling, and said the priest need not remain, and perhaps the gondolier had best return and watch my easel ; the good mother need not be alarmed. There was some mistake. She would return to the church with the painter and verify the good priest's story.

I stopped for a moment as she made her devotions at the altar. As we reached the outer door she caught sight of the jib, and stood still as if shocked. My yellow rag was waving in the sunlight as defiant as a matador's cloak !

Stooping under the improvised awning, she closely examined the sketch. How long would it take to finish it ? Half an hour. Be quick about it, then. If I did not mind, she would watch me paint. She stood for a long time without speaking, and then said, —

" Would not a touch of rose madder help that shadow ? "

" You paint, then ? " I asked, following her suggestion.

" I did once," she replied, and turned her head sadly and looked out over the blue lagoon towards San Giorgio.

An hour later she watched Ingenio and the

fisherman take down the jib and return it to the boat. But she would not receive my thanks. All artists were her friends. The sail made no difference, the sun was too hot to work without it, and she understood it all when she saw the sketch. She would close the church door. I need not wait. I drifted slowly out into the lagoon and looked back. She was still standing in the archway, shading her eyes with her hand, and watching us.

Then the fishing-boats spread their sails, drifted past, and shut her from my sight. Ingenio's cry of warning as he rounded a turn in the canal awoke me from my reverie. I picked up my sketch and stepped ashore. I will give it to any one who will tell me the history of that good gray nun.

A SUMMER'S DAY IN VENICE

BELOW the Piazza and quite near the Public Garden there is a small wine shop, the open door of which is covered by a striped awning of red and orange. Underneath this at all times of the day and most of the night are collected a group of Italians, who have one object in life which they never lose sight of, — never to do to-day what they can possibly do to-morrow or the next week. If time is money, the average Venetian is a millionaire. He has stored up for present and future use such a vast amount of leisure that it makes a busy man envious to contemplate him.

If you leave your gondola and cross the sunbaked quay to this shelter, these aristocrats will make room for you at their table and hand you a flagon of tepid water and a saucer containing two lumps of sugar; or perhaps the landlord will bring you a bottle of *cerise* (cherry juice) and a thin cigar about the size and length of a shoestring. The cigar has a movable backbone of a single broom straw.

Inside of this retreat are small tables, around which are seated other nabobs drinking coffee and playing dominoes. Occasionally one will rise from his seat, approach a high table at one end of the room, select a small bit of dried fish from a pewter platter, and gravely resume his chair with the air of a man who really owns the whole fish, but allows the landlord to keep it on his sideboard merely as a mark of the high esteem in which he holds him.

Should you land immediately opposite the awning and the open door, so as to be quite within sight from the inside, one of these princes will slide from his seat very much as a turtle does from his log and hold your boat steady with his staff until you step ashore. For this service you give him one penny, and quite a small penny at that.

A turn of Ingenio's wrist whirled the sharp blade of my gondola close to this quay one lovely morning in August, with results to me exactly similar to what I have described, and in a moment more I was dropping my second lump into the clumsy little cup which the land-lord filled from the common pot.

What to paint to-day was the question that bothered me. Should I go back to the Rialto and try the flight of steps up from the canal, with the gondolas and boats in the foreground, or the view from the Piazzetta across the small fruit market with the Great Bridge in the distance, or should I keep on to the Public Gardens and catch the fishing-boats as they came across from the Lido?

Ingenio stood by, hat in hand, trying to read my thoughts. It is delightful to watch him. He starts off with a great show of enthusiasm, points up the canal, seizes a cup, turns it upside down, plants a fork beside it, and by this pantomime seeks to recall to me a spot in yesterday's excursion where I halted long enough to make some memoranda of a cluster of mooring piles, with the round dome of the Salute in the distance.

"No? Bah! Certainly not; how stupid of me!" (All this in his face, for his native tongue is still unintelligible to me.) "That would be impossible. Then how about this?" And then follows another arrangement of saucers for sails, lumps of sugar for steps, and other breakfast accessories illustrating minor details which make it very plain to me that the spot in his mind *now* is lower down the Riva where the fishermen tie their boats to the staircase. This, after all, is really the only spot in Venice worthy the consideration of a great painter on so charming a morning as this.

But I did not want the staircase, and Ingenio saw it. I did, however, want another cup of coffee, and this he brought me.

But where to go, and what to paint! I have learned never to attempt to solve any difficulties in Venice, — I fall back on my gondolier.

A section of the Venetian Committee of Finance followed me to my gondola, and a modern Dives added one half of one penny to his worldly store steadying my boat. Ingenio bent to his oar, we glided along the edge of the quay, and I looked back. My gondolier had solved the problem. I would paint the wine shop. My eye had caught the flat quay protected by the marble railing, the glare of the white wall against the deep blue sky, the arching stairway, the soft, filmy outline of the Salute in the distance, and, centring the whole composition, the brilliant-colored awning casting its rich shadow, in which were dotted the groups of wealthy capitalists with the unlimitable bank account of interminable leisure.

An obliging row of houses served as an umbrella and cast a grateful shadow, upon the

218

edge of which I planted my easel. In five minutes more I was working away with as much
gusto as if I had planned to paint this identical
wine shop weeks before.

The usual Venetian crowd collected and
looked over my shoulder. The woman carrying
her two copper water pails slung to a light yoke,
and which she had filled at the fountain in the
Piazzetta adjoining ; the girls stringing beads ;
the fishermen carrying their nets to the boats
moored below ; another painter with his trap —
etiquette forbids him the privilege of the masses,
but all the same I am conscious that he slackens his pace and edges as near as he can, and
tiptoes himself for a glance ; the tangle-haired
children with abbreviated clothing and faces
like Raphael's cherubs ; the old hags shuffling
along in their heelless shoes ; the fat priest in
his sandals, and the pretty flower-girl in a costume not her own, — all these types are well
known to the painter in Venice.

Out on the canal I hear the shouts of the gondoliers and boatmen. My limited knowledge of
their language prevents my understanding what
the controversy is about, but all the boatmen
on both sides of the water have a voice in it,
and I am convinced from the way in which they
emphasize some of their expressions that their

dialect is punctuated by a very choice variety of profanity.

In the midst of this Babel, which is suddenly increased by the arrival of a number of fruit and fish venders, I hear a strain of music, sung with such a full, free, whole-souled sort of voice that it drowns all other sounds and instantly catches my ear : —

" Jammo, jammo neoppa, jammo ja."

Over the bridge it comes, and in a moment more I catch sight of the singer as he mounts the steps. First his red cap perched on the back of his head, crowning a mass of jet-black hair ; then his sunburned face, blue shirt open from the throat to the waist, red sash, and white trousers ; and then, as he descends on my side of the bridge, I notice that he is barefooted. A roar of laughter greets him as he halts at the wine shop, and follows him as he makes his way towards the crowd around my easel. Before he reaches me he breaks out again : —

" Jammo, jammo neoppa, jammo ja.
Funiculi funiculà funiculi funiculà."

Everybody about me welcomes him. The flower-girl gives him a rose, and one of the girls stringing beads a kiss ; the old woman a scolding, at which he laughs and makes a grimace, which instantly puts her in a good humor again. As he nears my easel he picks up a child, pinches it, and, when it cries, kisses it and puts it down. Then he plants himself immediately in front of me, completely hiding my view, and cranes his neck trying to see my sketch upside down. He is not impertinent or rude or aggressive ; he only wants to see what is going on.

I mildly expostulate, and the crowd break out against him in a chorus; and when he cannot be made to understand that he is very much in my way and very much out of his, Ingenio turns up and leads him gently to the rear. Then he sees it all, laughs until the quay rings, pats me on the back, and apologizes like a gentleman.

Before I can reply he dodges into a hallway opposite, hauls out a great seine, spreads it on the marble flagging of the Piazzetta, and falls to mending it with a will, singing at the top of his voice, and stopping every few moments to argue with the girl who is making lace behind her pot of flowers in the balcony over the way, or chaff some gondolier landing at the quay on his left, or send some witticism flying after a passer-by, to the intense delight of the whole community.

This went on for hours, I painting quietly,

and this breezy, happy-hearted, barefooted, sunburned, rosy-cheeked fisherman keeping the whole place alive and awake. Finally, he gathered up the net just as I finished washing my brushes, stowed it away in his boat near by, waved his hand to me, returned to his house and brought out a table, two chairs, and a bottle of Chianti wine, and without a moment's hesitation, crossed to where I was packing my sketch-trap, strapped it himself, locked his arm through mine, and led me to his table, his honest, handsome face saying as plain as could be told, " Come, comrade, we have had a hard day's work ; now let us have a bottle together." And we did.

I never see a bottle of Chianti but I think of this sunny fisherman, and I never drink one but I pledge him a bumper. I send him my greeting over the sea, and long life to him, and a wife to love him, and plenty of fish, and plenty of Chianti, and one bottle always for me ! I owe him my thanks for his hearty laugh, and his song, and his courtesy, and for his share in making this summer's day the pleasantest I spent in Venice.

THE TOP OF A GONDOLA

WHILE I am at breakfast this morning a fleet of lighter boats sweep slowly past my garden and moor to a cluster of piles off the Dogana.

I have been on the lookout for this picturesque flotilla for some time, and Ingenio knows it. Before I have half finished my omelette he arrives off the marble steps, and rounds in his gondola, steadying her against the incoming tide with one hand and waving his congratulations with the other.

One peculiarity of this gentle, loyal soul is the intense personal interest he takes in my affairs. When I am satisfied with my day's work Ingenio is bubbling over with happiness, and hums to himself as he rows along some old song, or rather one line of it. When my sky becomes muddy, or my shadows opaque, and I irritable and disgusted (what painter is not so sometimes?) poor Ingenio pulls away mute and sad, and comes forward every now and then with an anxious expression upon his face and watches

223

the sketch as if it was a sick child and I the physician upon whom its life depended.

This morning he is as happy over the arrival of these golden-winged boats from beyond the Lido as if he was my man Friday crying, "A sail!" and I his shipwrecked master.

In five minutes we are off, and running under the shadow of the Salute. As it is too hot to work in the sun, moored to a spile on the Canal, I direct Ingenio to the broad landing of the church, hoping to find some spot where I can put up my easel and umbrella and paint the group of lighters in comfort and at my leisure.

I convey this information with my umbrella staff, very much as a Londoner directs and stops a hansom cab with his walking-stick. Ingenio sees the point (of the staff, of course) over the edge of my gondola's awning, darts in among a number of fishing-boats, and immediately begins a search in the pavement of the Piazzetta for a crack wide and deep enough in which to anchor my umbrella and still keep sight of the lighters.

This combination proved difficult. There were cracks enough, and views enough; the problem was to utilize them together.

It is true, there was also a long, cool shadow slanting across the marble pavement which would serve as an umbrella, and which for a time was tempting, but sober second thought convinced me that it could not be depended on. It was not the shadow of the great dome of the Salute, but of one of its small towers; and the sun, in his mad climb to the zenith, was fast melting it up.

But if the shadow failed me Ingenio did not, for at that instant he returned from a search after narrow cracks with news of some wide openings. These proved to be half a dozen or more *félzi* laid up for the summer on the far side of the landing, under which I could crawl and so escape the heat.

The discovery so pleased my faithful gondolier that, without waiting for any instructions from me, he picked up the traps and deposited them in front of a row of great black beetles sprawled out on the pavement, apparently sunning themselves. On closer inspection they proved to be the tops of gondolas used in wet and wintry weather, whose owners, having no immediate use for them, had laid them by for a rainy day, like their extra pennies.

I inspected each one in turn, found one larger than the others, commanding a capital view of the boats, and crawled in at once.

It made a delightful studio, was just high enough and wide enough, and had two windows

225

on each side, with sliding shutters and sash like a cab's, which proved admirable in managing the light on my canvas.

The result was that I spent the whole day under its shelter, and finally completed my picture, Ingenio bringing me, from one of the fishing-boats, some broiled fish and a pot of coffee for luncheon, which I shared with him, he occupying the adjoining *félze*, and pushing his cup under mine for me to fill.

When the sun went down and I began packing up my traps, a number of gondoliers arrived, one of whom, a forbidding-looking fellow with a shock of red hair, informed Ingenio that the *félze* belonged to his gondola, and that he demanded eight *lira* for the use of it. On my replying that he could not earn one quarter of that amount with his *whole* gondola, and that one *lira*, which I handed him, would be more than a reasonable rent for his stationary sunshade, at best but *half* a gondola, he flew into a great rage, and tossed the *lira* back to Ingenio. Then finding that I paid no further attention to him and moved off, he collected a crowd of gondoliers, who, uniting their cries to his, jumped into their boats, and followed my own to the water-stairs of my lodgings, the whole mob shouting and gesticulating wildly.

There we were met by the porter. He is rather a thin gentleman, with a high forehead, and is proverbial for his politeness. As his entire life is spent on the front steps helping people in and out of their gondolas, it is deserved. He performed that service for me, and then turned upon the howling mob.

It was simply delightful to see the way he handled them. They evidently knew him and respected either his authority or patronage, — the latter probably.

During the discussion I sought the quiet of the garden, followed by Ingenio, who vented his indignation upon the whole crew, being especially severe upon the gentleman with the auburn locks, whom he described by gestures of infinite disgust.

Before long the porter sought me out, and explained that these gondoliers were a rough set, and that if I valued my peace of mind while in Venice I ought to make some settlement of the affair, and either pay the amount demanded or explain the circumstances to the other gondoliers.

At this juncture an idea occurred to me which I proceeded to put into practice.

I would invite the plaintiff and half a dozen of his confrères into the garden, install the porter as chief justice, and argue the case before him.

This programme was immediately carried out, — the porter acting in the double capacity of interpreter and judge.

The gondolier opened the case. He stated that he had been at work all day, and being too poor to pay some one to watch his *félze*, had left it unguarded. On his return, in the evening, he had surprised this rich painter as he was leaving it, who, after occupying it all day, had refused to pay for the privilege, except in a coin of so little value that it was almost an insult to the profession to offer it.

On the cross-examination it was shown that at this season of the year there were several hundred *félzi* decorating the vacant quays, landings, and piazzas of Venice (there being no back yards in which to store them) ; that a gondola had a summer and a winter top, consequently only one was or could be used at the same time ; and that now, in summer time, the *félze* I had occupied was of about as much use to the plaintiff as two umbrellas on a rainy day.

It was also shown that the gross earnings of a gondolier and a gondola combined average less than six *lira* a day, and that there was no instance on record in Venice or elsewhere in

which any gondolier had ever collected any
large or small amount of money for the use of
a *félže* for any period of time, long or short.

On the re-direct, the plaintiff wanted the
judge and jury to remember that no bargain
had been made for the use of the *félže ;* that
accordingly he had a right to charge what he
considered would compensate him, especially
since there existed no tariff for laid-by *félži,*
and that, in defiance of his rights of ownership,
I had forcibly entered and taken possession.

The effect of this last shot on the jury was
very pronounced. They looked at each other
wisely, and nodded concurrence.

It was now my turn, and as I was conducting my own case I summed up for the defence.

I asked the jury whether Italy was not now
free, and whether Venice was not a city free to
her citizens and to the strangers within her
gates. I reminded them that the days of Austrian tyranny were days of the past, and that
any Italian who would wish to renew them
would be a traitor to his country.

In those days a tax was placed upon the people of Venice so severe that the privations it
caused were still fresh in their memories.

Now, thanks to a humane government under
a wise king, all such onerous burdens had been

lifted from the people. Venice had a free harbor, free canals, free churches, piazzas, and landings.

How came it, then, that this plaintiff, representing so loyal a body of hard-working citizens as the gondoliers, should seek to bring back the days of tyranny and wrong?

The king had said these piazzas were free, and under this ruling I, a stranger, in the peaceful pursuit of my profession, had taken up my position in one of them. I had really occupied the pavement, not the *félze* [sensation], and if its top happened to be over me and so shaded me from the heat of the sun, that circumstance gave the plaintiff no more ground for charging me eight *lira* for its use than it did the owner of a palace who happened to own the shady side of the street, and so charged passers-by for the relief it afforded them.

This settled it. The judge decided in favor of the defendant, maintaining that *félzi* and Venice were free, and that the only charge which could reasonably be made would be against the gondolier for obstructing the painter and annoying him while engaged in the peaceful pursuit of his profession.

Ingenio afterwards reported that the verdict was entirely satisfactory to the jury, and also to the gondolier, who had not seen it in that light before.

When I saw him the next day and handed him again the one *lira*, he touched his hat and said, "Grazie, signore."

Since this little incident I have been more than ever impressed with the majesty of the law, which somehow or other always seems to protect me in these my wanderings.

BEHIND THE RIALTO

I AM at work painting an old bridge spanning a narrow canal which flows behind the Rialto. It is the sole dependence of a crooked crevice of a street which it helps over and across a sluggish waterway and into a small open square facing a church. This bridge also provides shop space for a vender of cheap pottery, whose wares of green and red glisten in the sun, supplying a spot of brilliant color to my composition. I know this church and its quaint interior, and I also know the caffè next to it, for here Ingenio and I often breakfast. It is an unpretentious place, but the coffee is always good, and sometimes the landlord serves a cutlet sliced quite thin and smothered in an inviting sauce.

This morning I prefer breakfasting in my gondola, and so send Ingenio for coffee and whatever else he can bring me from a larder rarely overstocked.

If you have never breakfasted in a gondola moored under the windows of an old palace, on its cool side, with your curtains drawn back, the water gurgling about you and reflecting the thousand tints of marble walls, white sails, and blue skies, I commend it to you as an experience which, once enjoyed, you will never forget.

When Ingenio returns with the coffee he brings me a message from the landlord, " that he is cooking a cutlet, and will send it to the bridge." Later on, in looking from between my curtains, I see a pale-faced child, scarce ten years of age, carrying between her outstretched hands a covered dish. I notice, also, that Ingenio helps her carefully down the slippery steps of the landing, relieves her of the cutlet, and when she hesitates and is timid about returning, picks her up gently in his arms, and places her safely on the quay at the entrance of the crevice of a street, through which she disappears, waving her hand.

In my experience gondoliers are not in the habit of exhibiting such watchful care over the youth of Venice, and so I ask Ingenio, in our sign language, now quite well understood between us, if the child belongs to him.

The old man smiles sadly, and a far-away look comes into his eyes ; then he shakes his head.

The cutlet and sketch finished, the gondola is headed up the canal, and Ingenio and I begin our daily search for good bric-à-brac at poor prices. To-day I want a staff, or boat-hook, similar to one I saw yesterday in the hands of a Venetian gentleman of unlimited leisure, who used it in steadying the gondola of an Englishman of unlimited means, who upon alighting immediately purchased it. It was studded all over with copper coins of various dates and diameters nailed to the wood, a kind of portable savings bank, and was altogether a very curious and interesting exhibit of Venetian life.

Ingenio thinks he knows a gondolier who may still own one. He is to be found at the right-hand landing of the Rialto. So we twist our way in and out of the narrow waterways, and under many bridges, and then through the broad water of the Grand Canal, spanned by the famous arch. But Ingenio's friend could not be found at the landing, or anywhere else in the vicinity, so we try another bridge lower down, and not finding him there, give up the search in this direction. A shop near the fish-market, another in one of the streets near the Piazzetta, and a fisherman's house above it, were next visited without success. Then Ingenio tells me he thinks he can find a staff near his own home, but a short distance away. Might he turn the gondola into the canal to our left ?

He had often before asked me to visit his home. At one time, it was because of a caffè opposite his house where they made an excellent omelette ; again, it was a cabinet-maker, who kept his shop near where he lived, and who had some old engravings in black frames. To-day, it is this much sought-for staff.

Until now either want of time or some more interesting excursion had always prevented my consenting, and when I again refuse, the same sad expression I often see passes over his face, and so, to please him, I nod my head. A few quick strokes bring us to an angle in the canal running behind the Rialto, and quite near where I had breakfasted in the morning.

A pleasant-faced woman, prematurely old, comes down a flight of steps built under a culvert-shaped arch, and holds the boat to the lower step. It is Ingenio's wife. I follow her under the arch, up a tottering flight of steps, and into a small, scrupulously clean room with high ceiling. It is their living room, and like all Venetian kitchens has its fireplace built out from the wall, while on either side of the raised hearth, two small windows, about one foot

235

square, look out on the canal. The shelf over the hearth and the wall above it shine with well polished brass and copper pans. White curtains soften the glare of the sunlight. Some pictures of the Holy Mother, a cheap crucifix, and a few articles of furniture complete the interior. Ingenio enters, having moored the gondola, gives me the best chair, draws the curtains that I may see the view of the Grand Canal and the Rialto, officiates as sign-interpreter between me and his wife, and then disappears into an adjoining room, leaving the door ajar. The good wife rises quickly and closes it behind him. As she regains her seat she says something to me in Italian which I do not understand.

In a moment more the door reopens and Ingenio enters, carrying in his arms a pale, hollow-cheeked child, about ten years of age, who looks at me wonderingly with her great round eyes. One hand is wound around her father's neck, her thin fingers lost in his bushy gray beard. The other holds a short crutch. I shall never forget the tender way in which the old man placed her on a low stool at his side, caressing her hair, holding fast her hand, and talking to her in a low undertone in his soft Italian; nor the tremor in his voice when he leaned over to me and said, pointing to his crippled daughter, —

"This one belongs to me."

It was all the child he had, poor fellow. She filled his heart full with her bright face and loving ways, and although she was his greatest sorrow, he was proud of her, and proud that I had seen her. Several years ago she had fallen from one of the bridges, struck a passing boat, and broken her thigh. Since then she had lived in these two rooms.

I understood now why he had lifted ashore so tenderly my little waitress with the cutlet.

When I regained my gondola I reminded Ingenio of the object of our search. Was the man at home? Had he seen the staff? Would he bring it to the boat? He hung his head, and did not move.

Then it all came out. There was no man with a gondola staff. There had been no cabinet-maker next door, with rare old engravings in black frames, nor any caffès with toothsome omelettes.

It was Giulietta he wanted me to see.

Patient, loyal, gentle old gondolier! With me you will forever be a part of sunny skies, old palaces, and the silver shimmer of the Lido, the bright sails of red and gold, the cool of dim, incense-laden churches, and crooked canals under quaint bridges.

Even now I hear your warning cry as you round the sharp corners of the canals. But I love best to remember you with that pale-faced child in your arms.

ESPERO GORGONI, GONDOLIER

POOR old Ingenio — my gondolier of five years ago — dear old Ingenio, with his white hair and gentle voice; Ingenio with the little crippled daughter and the sad-faced wife, who lived near the church behind the Rialto, had made his last crossing. At least the sacristan shook his head and pointed upward when I sought tidings of him; and the old, familiar door with the queer gratings was locked, and the windows cobwebbed and dust-begrimed.

None of the gondoliers at the Rialto landing knew, nor did any of the old men at the water-steps — the men with the hooked staffs who steady your boat while you alight. Five years was so very long ago, they said, and then there had been the plague.

So I looked up wistfully at the windows of the old palace where I had called to him so often — I can see him now, with little Giulietta in his arms, peering at me through the gay, climbing flowers which she watered so carefully — looked long and wistfully, as if he must

239

surely answer back, " Si, signore, subito," and turned sadly away.

But then there was the same old gondola landing, blue poles, bridge, and all, with its flock of gondolas hovering around, and a dozen lusty fellows ready to spring to their oars and serve me night and day for a pittance that else-where a man would starve on. My lucky star once sent me Ingenio, who floating past caught my signal ; why not another ?

This is why I am on the quay near the Rialto this lovely morning, in Venice, overlooking the gondolas curving in and out, and watching the faces of the gondoliers as with uplifted hands, like a row of whips, they call out their respec-tive numbers and qualifications.

In my experience there is nothing like a gon-dola to paint from, especially in the summer — and it is the summer time. Then all these Venetian cabs are gay in their sunshiny attire, and have laid aside their dark hooded cloaks, their rainy-day mackintoshes — their *félzi* — and have pulled over their shoulders a frail awn-ing of creamy white, with snowy draperies at sides and back, under which you paint in state or lounge luxuriously, drinking in the beauty about you.

ESPERO GORGONI, GONDOLIER

I have in my wanderings tried all sorts of moving studios : *tartanas* in Spain, *volantes* in Cuba, broad-sailed luggers in Holland, mules in Mexico, and cabs everywhere. One I remember with delight — an old night-hawk in Amsterdam — that offered me not only its front seat for my easel, its arm-rest for my water bottle, and a pocket in the door flap for brushes (I am likely to expect all these conveniences in even the most disreputable of cabs), but insisted on giving me the additional luxury of a knot-hole in its floor for waste water.

But with all this a cab is not a gondola.

In a gondola you are never shaken by the tired beast resting his other leg, nor by the small boy who looks in at the window, nor by the cabby, who falls asleep on the box and awakes periodically with a start that repeats a shiver through your brush hand, and a corresponding wave-line across your sky.

In place of this there is only a cosey curtain-closed nest, — a little boudoir with down cushions and silk fringes and soft morocco coverings ; kept afloat by a long, lithe, swan-like, moving boat, black as an Inquisitor's gown save for the dainty awning. A something bearing itself proudly with head high in air, — alive or still, alert or restful, and obedient to your lightest touch, — half sea-gull revelling in the sunlight, half dolphin cutting the dark water.

If you are hurried, and the plash of the oar comes quick and strong, in an instant your gondola quivers with the excitement of the chase. You feel the thrill through its entire length as it strains every nerve ; the touch of the oar, like the touch of the spur, urging it to its best. If you would rest, and so slip into some dark water-way under the shadow of overhanging balcony or mouldy palace wall, your water-swallow becomes a very *lasagnone*, and will go sound asleep, and for hours, or loll lazily, the little waves lapping about its bow.

In Venice my gondola is always my home, and my gondolier always my best friend ; and so when my search for Ingenio ended only in a cobwebbed door and an abandoned balcony, and that mournful shake of the sacristan's head, and I stood scanning anxiously the upturned faces below me, it was some minutes before I selected his successor and returned Espero's signal.

I cannot say why I singled him out except, perhaps, that he did not press forward with the rest, rushing his bow ahead ; but rather held back, giving his place to a gray-headed old gondolier, who in his haste had muffed his oar awkwardly, at which the others laughed.

Perhaps, too, it might have been his frank, handsome young face, with its merry black eyes; or the inviting look of the cushions beneath the white awning, with the bit of a rug on the floor; or the picturesque effect of the whole; or all of them together, that caught my eye. Or it might have been the perfect welding together of man and boat. For, as he stood erect in the sunlight, twisting the gondola with his oar, his loose shirt, with throat and chest bare, in highest light against the dark water, his head bound with a red kerchief, his well-knit, graceful figure swaying in the movement of the whole, — blending with and yet controlling it, — both man and boat seemed but parts of one organism, a sort of marine centaur, as free and fearless as that wonderful myth of the olden time. Whatever it was, my lucky star peeped out at the opportune moment, and the next instant my sketch-traps were tumbled in.

" To the Salute ! "

The gondolier threw himself on his oar, the sensitive craft quivered at the touch, and we glided out upon the broad waters of the Grand Canal.

Nowhere else in the wide world is there such a sight. A double row of creamy white palaces tiled in red and topped with quaint chimneys.

ESPERO GORGONI, GONDOLIER

Overhanging balconies of marble, fringed with flowers, with gay awnings above and streaming shadows below. Two lines of narrow quays crowded with people flashing bright bits of color in the blazing sun. Swarms of gondolas, *barche*, and lesser water-spiders darting in and out. Lazy red-sailed luggers, melon-loaded, with crinkled green shadows crawling beneath their bows ; while at the far end over the glistening highway, beaded with people, curves the beautiful bridge — an ivory arch against a turquoise sky.

Espero ran the gauntlet of the skimming boats, dodging the little steamers puffing away all out of breath with their run from the Lido, shot his boat into a narrow canal, and out again upon the broad water, until the edge of her steel blade touched the water-stairs of the Salute.

This beautiful church is always my rendezvous. It is halfway to everything, — to the Public Garden ; across the Giudecca ; away over to the Lagoon where the fishermen live ; to the Rialto and beyond.

In the freshness of the morning, when its lovely dome throws a cool shadow across its piazza, there is no better place for a painter to make up his mind as to where he would work. Mine required but a few minutes ; I would paint near the Fondimenta della Pallada ; a narrow, short canal where the fishermen moor their boats.

" What is your name, gondolier ? "

" Espero Gorgoni."

The voice was sweet and musical, and the answer was given with a turn of the head as graceful as it was free.

" Do you know the Pallada ? "

" Perfectly."

" Stop, then, where the crab baskets are moored to the poles."

A turn of the wrist, a long, bending sweep of the oar across the Giudecca, and we enter a water-way leading to the Lagoon. Here live the fishermen, in great, rambling houses three and four stories high, — warehouses probably in the old days, — running sheer into the water. Outside of the lower windows lie their boats, with gay-colored sails, and next to these stand a row of poles anchoring the huge wicker crab and fish baskets filled with their early morning catch.

Espero ran the gondola behind a protecting sail, and in five minutes I was at work.

The experience was not new to him. I saw that from the way he opened the awning on the proper side, unstrapped my easel, and spread out the contents of my trap on the cushions, which he reversed to protect from waste water ; and from the way he stepped ashore, so that my gondola should lie perfectly still, joining later a group of children who were watching me from the doorway above. (Half an hour after they were laughing at his stories, the two youngest in his lap.) A considerate, good-natured fellow, I thought, — this gondolier of mine, — and fond of children ; and I kept at work.

When the fisherman awoke and came down to make ready his boat for the morning, and I began the customary protest about the lowering of the sail, thus spoiling my sketch, Espero sprang up, locked his arm through that of the intruder, and led him gently back into the house, calling to me, five minutes thereafter, from across the canal, to keep at work and not to hurry, as the fisherman and he would have a mouthful of wine together. And a man of tact, too ! Really, if my gondolier develops like this, I shall not miss Ingenio so much.

The next day we were across the Lagoon, and the day following up the Giudecca, by the storehouses where the lighters unload ; and before the week was out I had fallen into my old habits and was sharing my breakfast and my cigarette-case with my gondolier, who, day by

day, won his way by some new trait of useful-
ness or some new charm of manner.

Oh, these breakfasts in the gondola in the
early morning ; the soft, fresh air of the sea in
your face, the cool plash of the water in your
ears !   On the floor of the boat, smoking hot,
rests the little copper coffee-pot ; above in the
wooden side-pockets, your store of fruit and
rolls.   With what a waste and recklessness is
the melon split and quartered, and the half-
eaten crescents thrown overboard !   What
savory fish !   What delicious bread !   What luscious figs !   And yet Espero had gathered them
all up at a caffè, a fruit-stand, and a baker's ;
and a bit of silver no larger than my thumb-
nail had paid for it all.

When the wind freshens and the boats from
Chioggia begin spreading their sails, Espero
turns his prow toward the Public Gardens, —
their mooring-ground, — and we follow them
out over the broad water until my sketch-book
is filled with their varying forms and colors.
On our way back we board the wood-boats,
drifting in with the tide, or land under the
old garden walls, which Espero scales, regaining the gondola loaded with flowers, which
he festoons over the awning, trailing the blos-

soming vines in the water behind. Or we circle about the Salute, composing it now on the right, with some lighter boats in the distance; now on the left, with the Dogana and the stretch of palaces beyond. Or we haunt the churches, listening to the music, or follow with our eyes the slender, graceful Venetians who come and go.

In all these rambles there was one little, crooked canal near the Salute that, whatever our course, Espero always dodged into. Long way around or short way over, it was always the same. Somehow Espero must get into this water-way to get out somewhere else. At last I caught him. She wore a yellow silk handkerchief tied under her pretty chin, and was waving her hand from a balcony filled with oleanders high up on the wall of a crumbling old palace. These were our days!

Then came the twilights, with palace, tower, and dome purple in the fading light, the canal all molten gold, the gondolas, with lamps alight, gliding like fireflies.

On one of these purple-laden twilights we had floated over to San Giorgio, moored the gondola to a great iron ring in the water-soaked steps that might once have held a slave-laden galley, and had sat down to watch the darkness as it slowly settled over the dreaming city. Away off to the right stood the Campanile, its cone-shaped top pink and gold, while behind, against the deepening blue, rose its twin tower.

The scene awoke all the old memories, and I began talking to Espero, who was stretched out on the marble steps below me, of the olden times when this same harbor was full of ships of every clime, with sails of gold and cargoes of spice, and of the great regattas, and the two-decked war barges, with slaves double-banked rowing beneath; and from this to the wonderful Bucentaur, the Doge's barge, encrusted with gold, rowed by the members of the Arsenalotti, a sort of guild or corporation formed of the workmen at the Arsenal. How, every year, occurred the ceremony of the Espousal of the Adriatic, and how, when the Bucentaur returned, there was a grand banquet, at which the Arsenalotti dined at the public expense, with the privilege of carrying off everything on the table, even the linen, vessels, and glass.

Espero's attitude and face, as he listened, led me on. He had an odd way of lifting his eyebrows quickly when I told him something that interested him, — a questioning yet deferential expression, which I generally accepted

249

as a tribute to my superior intelligence. He never formulated it in words. It was only one of the many flashes that swept over his face, but it was always a grateful encouragement.

And so, with the glamour of the scene about me, and with Espero's eyes fastened on mine, his well-shaped head clear-cut against the fading sky, I rambled on, telling him of those things I thought would please him the most. Of how these Arsenalotti became gondoliers, joining the Castellani, — the gondoliers at that time being divided into two parties, the Castellani, who wore red hoods, and the Nicoletti, who wore black hoods. Of how these Castellani were aristocrats and had portioned out to them the eastern part of the city, where the Doge lived, his residence being in the Piazza of San Marco; while the Nicoletti were only publicans. That, besides attending to the Doge in public, many of these Castellani had served him in private, thus being of great service to the state.

Espero listened to every word, raising his head and looking at me curiously when I mentioned the Castellani, and laughing outright at my description of the banquet tables in the hands of the Arsenalotti. Nothing else dropped from his lips except the grim remark that if he had lived in those days he would, perhaps, have owned his own gondola, and not have had to use his grandfather's, who was now too old to row. I remembered afterward that a certain thoughtful expression overspread his face, as if my talk had awakened some memory of his own.

A passing music-boat cut short my dissertation, and in a moment more we were following in its wake, threading our way in and out of the tangle of gondolas massed about it. Then a twist of the oar, and Espero glided alongside the lantern-hung barge and leaned over to speak to the leader. The musicians were going to the Piazza, would I care to hear them sing under the Bridge of Sighs?

In five minutes we had picked our way through the labyrinth of surrounding gondolas, and in five more had entered the close, narrow canal, where the beautiful bridge, buttressed by two great masses of gloom, — the palace and the prison, — overhung the sluggish, sullen water.

There is never a lantern now along this weird and gruesome water-way. One only sees the twinkling lamps of the gondolas, like will-o'-the-wisps, drift past, — the boats themselves lost in the blackness of the shadows, — the glimmer of the pale light of some slow-moving barge, or the reflection of the stars above. All else is dark and ghostly.

The music-boat drifted sideways, and the bass viol, who was standing, twisted a light cord through an iron ring in the slimy, ooze-colored palace. Espero drifted against the opposite wall, the prison.

" What shall they sing, signore ? "

" As you please, Espero."

I have heard the Miserere chanted at dead of night in the streets of an old Italian town, the flare of the torches lighting the upturned face of the ghastly dead ; my eyes have filled when, with knee to marble floor, I have listened to the pathos of its harmonies sighing through the many-pillared mosque of Cordova ; I have drunk in its cadences in curtained alcoves with the breath of waving fans and flash of gems about me ; but never has its grandeur and majesty so stirred my imagination and entranced my soul as on this night in Venice, under the deep blue of the soft Italian sky, the frowning, blood-stained palace above, the treacherous, silent water beneath.

I could stretch out my hand and touch the very stones that had coffined the living dead. I could look down into the same depths along the edge of the water-soaked marble where had lain the headless body, with sack and cord, awaiting the sure current of the changing tide; and from my cushions in the listening gondola I could see, high up against the blue in the starlight, the same narrow window in the fatal arch, through which the hopeless had caught a last glimpse of light and life.

When the last low strains had died away, Espero raised himself erect, walked slowly the length of the gondola, and, bending down, said in a voice tremulous with emotion, " Signore, did you hear the tramp of the poor fellows over the bridge, and the moans of the men dying under the wall ? Holy God ! Was it not terrible ? "

At that instant the barge floated past. I looked at him in wonder, — Espero's eyes were full of tears !

This man began to interest me intensely. Only an every-day, plain, Venetian gondolier, in a blue shirt, and patched at that, with hardly a franc he could call his own, and yet there was something about him that made his presence a delight. It was not the graceful swing of his beautiful body, nor his musical laugh, nor his honest kindness to every human being. It was rather an undefined, courteous, well-bred independence.

When it came to rowing a gondola, it never seemed to me that he rowed because it was his duty and his livelihood. He rowed because he loved it, and because he loved the sunshine across his face and the flash of the water on his oar-blade — the swing and freedom of it all. My happening to be a passenger was but one of those necessary evils attending the earning and payment of five francs a day. And yet, not altogether an evil; for he loved me, too, as he did everything else that brought him companionship and air and light and life.

Nothing seemed to tire him. Day or night, or all night, if I wished it — for often we were whole nights together in the soft summer air, floating back to the sleeping city in the gray dawn, stopping to listen to early mass at the Pieta or following the fruit-boats or fishermen in from the Lido.

And thus it was that we ransacked Venice from San Giorgio to Murano; and thus it was that every day I caught some fresh glimpse of the sweetness of his inner nature, and every day loved him the better. Nobody could have helped it. There was that touch about him one could not resist. Once on the Giudecca when the sea was polished steel and the tide turning ebb, Espero ran the gondola up under the lee of a melon-boat, its sail limp and useless in the breathless air, sprang over her rail, caught the oar from the captain, fagged out with the long pull from the Lido, and threw his weight against the drooping blade. And all this with a laugh and a twist of his foot in pirouette, as if it was the merriest fun in the world to save a tide and a market for a man he had never seen in his life before.

On another morning he was just in time to save Beppo from a plunge overboard, — old Beppo, who for centuries (nobody knows how old Beppo is) has hooked his staff into myriads of gondolas landing at the Salute steps. It had happened that some other mediæval ruin, a few years Beppo's junior, had crowded the old man from his place, and Espero's righteous wrath was not appeased until he had driven the usurper from the piazza of the church, with the parting reminder that he would break every bone in his withered old skin if he ever caught him there again.

And yet, with all my opportunities for intimacy, I really got no nearer to the inner side of Espero than the day I hired him. To him I was still only the painter from over the sea, his patron, to whom he was loyal, good-natured, happy-hearted, and obliging ; but nothing more. Nothing more was for sale for five francs a day. What his home or life might be outside the hours I called my own, I knew no more than of the hundred other gondoliers who filled the canal with their cries and their laughter. The one sole connecting link was the pretty Venetian of the little, crooked canal, who waved her hand whenever we passed, and who once tossed down a spray of oleander which fell at his feet ; and yet I could not even have found her doorway, much less have told her name.

One beautiful, bright Sunday morning, perplexed at this unequal exchange of confidences, this idea took possession of me. Espero and I would breakfast together — blue shirt, patch, and all ! Not as we had often breakfasted before, in the gondola under the shadow of a palace, or down by the stalls of the fruit market ; but at the great Caffè Florian, in the Piazza of San Marco, at twelve o'clock, high noon, in the midst of gold embroidered officers with clanking swords and waxed mustaches, and ladies of high degree in dainty gowns and veils.

"Leave the gondola, Espero, in charge of somebody, and come with me ! "

We twisted our way through the narrow slits

of streets, choked with awnings shading groups of Venetians sipping their coffee, dodged under an archway, across a narrow bridge, and so out upon the blinding, baking Piazza, dotted here and there with hurrying figures, dogged by ink-spilled shadows.

"Breakfast for two!" I said to the startled waiter. "Take the seat by the window, Espero!"

His face lighted up, and an expression of the greatest happiness and good humor overspread it. But that was all. There was no sign of humility; nothing indicating that I had done him a kindness, or had conferred upon him any special favor. He merely pointed to himself, and then to the seat, as if making quite sure, saying, "Me, signor?" and then sat himself down, spreading his napkin, and all with the air of a man accustomed to that sort of thing every day of his life.

I ordered nearly everything on the bill of fare. Fish, eggs, salad, broiled cutlet, fruit, even a bottle of Chianti, with silk tassels on its neck. Espero took each in its course with the easy grace of a Chesterfield, and the quiet refinement of a man of the world.

The only person who put his astonishment into words was the head waiter, who caught his breath when I lighted Espero's cigarette myself, recounting to his assistant, and adding, " *Ma foi*, what funny people, these painters ! "

An hour later we were again afloat, embarking at the water-steps of the Piazza.

Just here, and for the first time in all our intercourse, I noticed a change in Espero's bearing. The touch of humility — it had been only a trace, and as I always knew, only assumed that I might see he recognized the obligation of five francs — even that slight touch was gone.

The change was not one that betokened presuming familiarity, as if all social barriers having now been swept away he would insist upon sharing with me everything I owned. It was more the manner of a man clothed with the responsibility of a host ; a welcoming, generous, appropriating manner. Heretofore, when I had stepped into the gondola, Espero invariably offered me his bent elbow to steady myself ; but now he gave me his hand.

Furthermore, he did not wait for instructions as to where the prow of the gondola should be pointed.   He said, instead, —

" There is a famous old Cortile that I must show you. All the artists paint it. We will go now ! "

With this he shot past our customary land-

258

ing place, entered the little crooked canal, and rounded the gondola in front of an old marble archway curiously carved.

I began to wonder at the change that had come over him. What was there about this Cortile ? If everybody had painted it, why should he have kept it hidden all summer from me ?

Espero's manner at this landing was, if anything, more expressive than at the last; for, after securing the gondola, he waved his hand graciously and led me along a damp, tunnel-like passage, until we stepped into an abandoned cloister, once the most beautiful Cortile in Venice.

When we entered the sun was blazing against the opposite wall, the nearer columns standing out strong and dark. In the square, bounded by the low wall supporting the pillars, which in turn supported the living-rooms above, climbing vines and grasses ran riot, while in the centre of the tangled mass of weeds stood an old covered well, at which a girl was filling her copper water-pail.

Espero watched my delight at its picturesqueness, laughing outright at my determination to begin work at once, and then, with great deference, led me to a doorway level with the flagging of the mouldy pavement. Here he rang a

259

bell hung on the outside. The next instant a shutter opened above and a pair of black eyes peered out from between some pots of oleanders. It was the same face I had seen so often smiling at Espero from an upper balcony ! The cloister evidently abutted on the little crooked canal. This, then, was what he was hiding ! But surely he could not have thought that I would have stolen his sweetheart.

Another moment and the door was opened by the same pretty Venetian, who ushered us into a square hall having a broad staircase which led to the floor above. Here, on the wainscoted walls, halfway to the ceiling, hung a collection of old portraits, each one a delight to the eye of a painter. They were of men costumed in the time of the later Doges, — one in scarlet and black, another in a robe of deep blue, while a third wore a semi-military uniform and carried a short sword.

They all had one distinguishing feature : each head was covered by a bright red hood.

Espero never took his eyes from my face as I looked about me in astonishment, not even long enough to salute the pretty Venetian who stood smiling at his side.

" Who lives here, Espero ? "

" My grandfather, signor, who is very old,

lives on this floor. My little wife, Mariana,"
turning to the pretty Venetian, "and I live on
the floor above ; " and he kissed the girl on
the forehead and laid her hand in mine.

" And these portraits " —

" Are some of the famous gondoliers of old.
This one was chief of the Arsenalotti, and an
intimate friend of the Doge."

" And the others ? "

Espero's eyes twinkled, and a quizzical, half-
triumphant smile broke over his face.

" These are all my ancestors, signor. We
have been gondoliers for two hundred years. I
am a Castellani ! "

THE END

The Riverside Press

Electrotyped and printed by H. O. Houghton & Co.
Cambridge, Mass., U. S. A.